HIS NAMES WERE MANY
HIS MISSIONS WERE IMPOSSIBLE

The first assignment was to find and destroy who-ever was attempting to sabotage a controversial nuclear project. That was tricky . . . because he would have to kill himself in the process!

The second was to clear a gang of dolphins of a murder charge. That was trouble . . . especially when it meant battling a scientist with homicidal tendencies!

The third was to arrange for the destruction of a quasi-human telefactor that had returned to Earth to destroy its four programmers. That was the killer . . . since old telefactors never die!

OTHER BOOKS BY ROGER ZELAZNY:

Creatures of Light and Darkness
The Dream Master
Four For Tomorrow
The Guns of Avalon
Lord of Light
Nine Princes in Amber
Sign of the Unicorn
This Immortal
To Die in Italbar

MY NAME IS LEGION

Roger Zelazny

BALLANTINE BOOKS • NEW YORK

Library of Congress Catalog Card Number: 75-44242

ISBN 0-345-24867-8-150

Cover art by The Brothers Hildebrandt

Manufactured in the United States of America

First Edition: April, 1976

To Bill Spangler and Fred Lerner;
for two very good reasons

CONTENTS

PART ONE

The Eve of RUMOKO

I was in the control room when the J-9 unit flaked out on us. I was there for purposes of doing some idiot maintenance work, among other things.

There were two men below in the capsule, inspecting the Highway to Hell, that shaft screwed into the ocean's bottom thousands of fathoms beneath us and soon to be opened for traffic. Ordinarily, I wouldn't have worried, as there were two J-9 technicians on the payroll. Only, one of them was on leave in Spitzbergen and the other had entered sick bay just that morning. As a sudden combination of wind and turbulent waters rocked the *Aquina* and I reflected that it was now the Eve of RU-MOKO, I made my decision. I crossed the room and re-moved a side panel.

"Schweitzer! You're not authorized to fool around with that!" said Doctor Asquith.

I studied the circuits, and, "Do *you* want to work on it?" I asked him.

"Of course not. I wouldn't know how to begin. But—"

"Do you want to see Martin and Demmy die?"

"You know I don't. Only you're not—"

"Then tell me who is," I said. "That capsule down there is controlled from up here, and we've just blown something. If you know somebody better fit to work on it, then you'd better send for him. Otherwise, I'll try to repair the J-9 myself."

He shut up then, and I began to see where the trouble

1

was. They had been somewhat obvious about things. They had even used solder. Four circuits had been rigged, and they had fed the whole mess back through one of the timers. . . .

So I began unscrewing the thing. Asquith was an oceanographer and so should know little about electronic circuits. I guessed that he couldn't tell that I was undoing sabotage. I worked for about ten minutes, and the drifting capsule hundreds of fathoms beneath us began to function once again.

As I worked, I had reflected upon the powers soon to be invoked, the forces that would traverse the Highway to Hell for a brief time, and then like the Devil's envoy —or the Devil himself, perhaps—be released, there in the mid-Atlantic. The bleak weather that prevails in these latitudes at this time of year did little to improve my mood. A deadly force was to be employed, atomic energy, to release an even more powerful phenomenon —live magma—which seethed and bubbled now miles beneath the sea itself. That anyone should play senseless games with something like this was beyond my comprehension. Once again, the ship was shaken by the waves.

"Okay," I said. "There were a few shorts and I straightened them out." I replaced the side panel. "There shouldn't be any more trouble."

He regarded the monitor. "It seems to be functioning all right now. Let me check. . . ."

He flipped the toggle and said, *"Aquina* to capsule. Do you read me?"

"Yes," came the reply. "What happened?"

"Short circuit in the J-9," he answered. "It has been repaired. What is your condition?"

"All systems returned to normal. Instructions?"

"Proceed with your mission," he said, then turned to me. "I'll recommend you for something or other," he said. "I'm sorry I snapped at you. I didn't know you could service the J-9."

"I'm an electrical engineer," I replied, "and I've studied this thing. I know it's restricted. If I hadn't been able to figure out what was wrong, I wouldn't have touched it."

"I take it you'd rather not be recommended for something or other?"

"That is correct."

"Then I will not do it."

Which was a very good thing, for the nonce, as I'd also disconnected a small bomb, which then resided in my left-hand jacket pocket and would soon be tossed overboard. It had had another five to eight minutes to go and would have blotted the record completely. As for me, I didn't even want a record; but if there had to be one, it would be mine, not the enemy's.

I excused myself and departed. I disposed of the evidence. I thought upon the day's doings.

Someone had tried to sabotage the project. So Don Walsh had been right. The assumed threat had been for real. Consume that and digest it. It meant that there was something big involved. The main question was, "What?" The second was, "What next?"

I lit a cigarette and leaned on the *Aquina*'s rail. I watched the cold north sea attack the hull. My hands shook. It was a decent, humanitarian project. Also, a highly dangerous one. Even forgetting the great risks, though, I could not come up with a good counterinterest. Obviously, however, there was one.

Would Asquith report me? Probably. Though he would not realize what he was doing. He would have to explain the discontinuance of function in the capsule in order to make his report jibe with the capsule's log. He would say that I had repaired a short circuit. That's all.

That would be enough.

I had already decided that the enemy had access to the main log. They would know about the disconnected bomb not being reported. They would also know who had stopped them; and they might be interested enough, at a critical time like this, to do something rash. Good. That was precisely what I wanted.

. . . Because I had already wasted an entire month waiting for this break. I hoped they would come after me soon and try to question me. I took a deep drag on the cigarette and watched a distant iceberg glisten in the sun. This was going to be a strange one—I had that feeling. The skies were gray and the oceans were dark. Somewhere, someone disapproved of what was going on here, but for the life of me I could not guess why.

Well, the hell with them all. I like cloudy days. I was born on one. I'd do my best to enjoy this one.

I went back to my cabin and mixed myself a drink, as I was then officially off duty.

After a time, there came a knocking on my door.

"Turn the handle and push," I said.

It opened and a young man named Rawlings entered.

"Mister Schweitzer," he said, "Carol Deith would like to speak with you."

"Tell her I'm on my way," I said.

"All right," and he departed.

I combed my sort of blond hair and changed my shirt, because she was pretty and young. She was the ship's Security Officer, though, so I had a good idea as to what she was really after.

I walked to her office and knocked twice on the door.

As I entered, I bore in mind the fact that it probably involved the J-9 and my doings of a half hour before. This would tend to indicate that she was right on top of everything.

"Hello," I said. "I believe you sent for me?"

"Schweitzer? Yes, I did. Have a seat, huh?" and she gestured at one on the other side of her expensive desk.

I took it.

"What do you want?"

"You repaired the J-9 this afternoon."

I shrugged. "Are you asking me or telling me?"

"You are not authorized to touch the thing."

"If you want, I can go back and screw it up and leave it the way I found it."

"Then you admit you worked on it?"

"Yes."

She sighed.

"Look, I don't care," she said. "You probably saved two lives today, so I'm not about to fault you for a security violation. What I want to know is something different."

"What?"

"Was it sabotage?"

And there it was. I had felt it coming.

"No," I said. "It was not. There were some short circuits—"

"Bull," she told me.

"I'm sorry. I don't understand—"

"You understand, all right. Somebody gimmicked that thing. You undid it, and it was trickier than a couple of short circuits. And there was a bomb. We monitored its explosion off the port bow about half an hour ago."

"You said it," I said. "I didn't."

"What's your game?" she asked me. "You cleaned up for us, and now you're covering up for somebody else. What do you want?"

"Nothing," I said.

I studied her. Her hair was sort of reddish and she had freckles, lots of them. Her eyes were green. They seemed to be set quite far apart beneath the ruddy line of her bangs. She was fairly tall—like five-ten—though she was not standing at the moment. I had danced with her once at a shipboard party.

"Well?"

"Quite well," I said. "And yourself?"

"I want an answer."

"To what?"

"Was it sabotage?"

"No," I said. "Whatever gave you that idea?"

"There have been other attempts, you know."

"No, I didn't know."

She blushed suddenly, highlighting her freckles. What had caused that?

"Well, there have been. We stopped all of them, obviously. But they were there."

"Who did it?"

"We don't know."

"Why not?"

"We never got hold of the people involved."

"How come?"

"They were clever."

I lit a cigarette.

"Well, you're wrong," I said. "There were some short circuits. I'm an electrical engineer and I spotted them. That was all, though."

She found one someplace, and I lit it for her.

"Okay," she said. "I guess I've got everything you want to tell me."

I stood then.

". . . By the way, I ran another check on you."

"Yes?"

"Nothing. You're clean as snow and swansdown."

"Glad to hear it."

"Don't be, Mister Schweitzer. I'm not finished with you yet."

"Try everything," I said. "You'll find nothing else." . . . And I was sure of that.

So I left her, wondering when they would reach me.

I send one Christmas card each year, and it is unsigned. All it bears—in block print—is a list of four bars and the cities in which they exist. On Easter, May Day, the first day of summer, and Halloween, I sit in those bars and sip drinks from nine until midnight, local time. Then I go away. Each year, they're different bars.

Always, I pay cash, rather than using the Universal Credit Card which most people carry these days. The bars are generally dives, located in out-of-the-way places.

Sometimes Don Walsh shows up, sits down next to me and orders a beer. We strike up a conversation, then take a walk. Sometimes he doesn't show up. He never misses two in a row, though. And the second time he always brings me some cash.

A couple of months ago, on the day when summer came bustling into the world, I was seated at a table in the back of the Inferno, in San Miguel de Allende, Mexico. It was a cool evening, as they all are in that place, and the air had been clean and the stars very bright as I walked up the flagstone streets of that national monument. After a time, I saw Don enter, wearing a dark, fake-wool suit and yellow sport shirt, opened at the neck. He moved to the bar, ordered something, turned and let his eyes wander about the tables. I nodded when he grinned and waved. He moved toward me with a glass in one hand and a Carta Blanca in the other.

"I know you," he said.

"Yeah, I think so. Have a seat?"

He pulled out a chair and seated himself across from me at the small table. The ashtray was filled to overflowing, but not because of me. The odor of tequila was on the breeze—make that "draft"—from the opened front of the narrow barroom, and all about us two-dimensional nudes fought with bullfight posters for wall space.

"Your name is . . . ?"

"Frank," I said, pulling it out of the air. "Wasn't it in New Orleans . . . ?"

"Yeah, at Mardi Gras—a couple years ago."

"That's right. And you're . . . ?"

"George."

"Right. I remember now. We went drinking together. Played poker all night long. Had a hell of a good time."

". . . And you took me for about two hundred bucks."

I grinned.

"So what've you been up to?" I asked him.

"Oh, the usual business. There are big sales and small sales. I've got a big one going now."

"Congratulations. I'm glad to hear that. Hope it works out."

"Me, too."

So we made small talk while he finished his beer; then, "Have you seen much of this town?" I asked.

"Not really. I hear it's quite a place."

"Oh, I think you'll like it. I was here for their Festival once. Everybody takes bennies to stay awake for the whole three days. *Indios* come down from the hills and put on dances. They still hold *paseos* here, too, you know? And they have the only Gothic cathedral in all of Mexico. It was designed by an illiterate Indian, who had seen pictures of the things on postcards from Europe. They didn't think it would stay up when they took the scaffolding down, but it did and has done so for a long time."

"I wish I could stick around, but I'm only here for a day or so. I thought I'd buy some souvenirs to take home to the family."

"This is the place. Stuff is cheap here. Jewelry, especially."

"I wish I had more time to see some of the sights."

"There is a Toltec ruin atop a hill to the northeast, which you might have noticed because of the three crosses set at its summit. It is interesting because the government still refuses to admit it exists. The view from up there is great."

"I'd like to see it. How do you get in?"

"You just walk out there and climb it. It doesn't exist, so there are no restrictions."

"How long a hike?"

"Less than an hour, from here. Finish your beer, and we'll take a walk."

He did, and we did.

He was breathing heavily in a short time. But then, he lived near sea level and this was like 6,500 feet, elevation.

We made it up to the top, though, and wandered amid cacti. We seated ourselves on some big stones.

"So, this place doesn't exist," he said, "the same as you."

"That's right."

"Then it's not bugged—no, it couldn't be—the way most bars are these days."

"It's still a bit of wilderness."

"I hope it stays this way."

"Me, too."

"Thanks for the Christmas card. You looking for a job?"

"You know it."

"All right. I've got one for you."

And that's how this one started.

"Do you know about the Leeward and Windward Islands?" he asked me. "Or Surtsey?"

"No. Tell me."

"Down in the West Indies—in the Lesser Antilles system—starting in an arc heading southeasterly from Puerto Rico and the Virgin Islands toward South America, are those islands north of Guadeloupe which represent the high points of a subterranean ridge ranging from forty to two hundred miles in width. These are oceanic islands, built up from volcanic materials. Every peak is a volcano—extinct or otherwise."

"So?"

"The Hawaiians grew up in the same fashion. —Surtsey, though, was a twentieth-century phenomenon: a volcanically created island which grew up in a very brief time, somewhat to the west of the Vestmanna Islands, near Iceland. That was in 1963. Capelinhos, in the Azores, was the same way, and had its origin undersea."

"So?" But I already knew, as I said it. I already knew about Project RUMOKO—after the Maori god of volcanoes and earthquakes. Back in the twentieth century, there had been an aborted Mohole Project and there had been natural-gas-mining deals which had involved deep drilling and the use of "shaped" atomic charges.

"RUMOKO," he said. "Do you know about it?"

"Somewhat. Mainly from the *Times* Science Section."

"That's enough. We're involved."

"How so?"

"Someone is attempting to sabotage the thing. I have been retained to find out who and how and why, and to stop him. I've tried, and have been eminently unsuccessful to date. In fact, I lost two of my men under rather strange circumstances. Then I received your Christmas card."

I turned toward him, and his green eyes seemed to glow in the dark. He was about four inches shorter than me and perhaps forty pounds lighter, which still made him a pretty big man. But he had straightened into a nearly military posture, so that he seemed bigger and stronger than the guy who had been wheezing beside me on the way up.

"You want me to move in?"

"Yes."

"What's in it for me?"

"Fifty thousand. Maybe a hundred fifty—depending on the results."

I lit a cigarette.

"What will I have to do?" I finally asked.

"Get yourself assigned as a crewman on the *Aquina* —better yet, a technician of some kind. Can you do that?"

"Yes."

"Well, do it. Then find out who is trying to screw the thing up. Then report back to me—or else take them out of the picture any way you see fit. *Then* report back to me."

I chuckled.

"It sounds like a big job. Who is your client?"

"A U.S. Senator," he said, "who shall remain name-less."

"With that I can guess," I said, "but I won't."

"You'll do it?"

"Yes. I could use the money."

"It will be dangerous."

"They all are."

We regarded the crosses, with the packs of cigarettes and other various goodies tied to them in the way of religious offerings.

"Good," he said. "When will you start?"

"Before the month is out."

"Okay. When will you report to me?"

I shrugged, under starlight.

"When I've got something to say."

"That's not good enough, this time. September 15 is the target date."

". . . If it goes off without a hitch?"

"Fifty grand."

"If it gets tricky, and I have to dispose of a *corpus* or three?"

"Like I said."

"Okay. You're on. Before September 15."

"No reports?"

". . . Unless I need help, or have something important to say."

"You may, this time."

I extended my hand.

"You've got yourself a deal, Don."

He bowed his head, nodding to the crosses.

"Give me this one," he finally said. "I want this one. The men I lost were very good men."

"I'll try. I'll give you as much as I can."

"I don't understand you, mister. I wish I knew how you—"

"Good. I'd be crushed if you ever knew how I."

And we walked back down the hill, and I left him off at the place where he was staying that night.

"Let me buy you a drink," said Martin, as I passed him on the foredeck on my way out of Carol Deith's cabin.

"All right," and we walked to the ship's lounge and had one.

"I've got to thank you for what you did while Demmy and I were down there. It—"

"It was nothing," I said. "You could have fixed it yourself in a minute if somebody else had been down and you'd been up here."

"It didn't work out that way, though, and we're happy you were handy."

"I consider myself thanked," I said, raising the plastic beer stein—they're all plastic these days. Damn it!

"What kind of shape was that shaft in?" I asked him.

"Excellent," he said, furrowing his wide, ruddy forehead and putting lots of wrinkles around his bluish eyes.

"You don't look as confident as you sound."

He chuckled then, took a small sip.

"Well, it's never been done before. Naturally, we're all a little scared. . . ."

I took that as a mild appraisal of the situation.

"But, top to bottom, the shaft was in good shape?" I asked.

He looked around him, probably wondering whether the place was bugged. It was, but he wasn't saying anything that could hurt him, or me. If he had been, I'd have shut him up.

"Yes," he agreed.

"Good," and I thought back on the sayings of the short man with the wide shoulders. "Very good."

"That's a strange attitude," he said. "You're just a paid technician."

"I take a certain pride in my work."

He gave me a look I did not understand, then, "That sounds strangely like a twentieth-century attitude."

I shrugged.

"I'm old-fashioned. Can't get away from it."

"I like that," he said. "I wish more people were that way, these days."

"What's Demmy up to, now?"

"He's sleeping."

"Good."

"They ought to promote you."

"I hope not."

"Why not?"

"I don't like responsibilities."

"But you take them on yourself, and you handle them well."

"I was lucky—once. Who knows what will happen, next time . . . ?"

He gave me a furtive look.

"What do you mean, 'next time'?"

"I mean, if it happens again," I said. "I just happened to be in the control room. . . ."

I knew then that he was trying to find out what I knew—so neither of us knew much, though we both knew that something was wrong.

He stared at me, sipped his beer, kept staring at me, then nodded. "You're trying to say that you're lazy?"

"That's right."

"Crap."

I shrugged and sipped mine.

Back around 1957—fifty years ago—there was a thing called AMSOC, and it was a joke. It was a takeoff on the funny names of alphabetized scientific organizations. It stood for the American Miscellaneous Society. It represented something other than a joke on the organization man, however. This was because Doctor Walter Munk of Scripps Institution of Oceanography and Doctor Harry Hess of Princeton were members, and they had come up with a strange proposal which later died for lack of funds. Like John Brown, however, while it lay moldering in its grave, its spirit kept shuffling its feet.

It is true that the Mohole Project died stillborn, but

that which eventually came of the notion was even grander and more creative.

Most people know that the crust of the Earth is twenty-five or more miles thick under the continents, and that it would be rough drilling there. Many also know that under the oceans the crust is much thinner. It would be quite possible to drill there, into the top of the mantle, penetrating the Mohorovicic Discontinuity, however. They had talked about all kinds of data that could be picked up. Well, okay. But consider something else: sure, it's true that a sampling of the mantle would provide some answers to questions involving radioactivity and heat flow, geological structure and the age of the Earth. Working with natural materials, we would know boundaries, thicknesses of various layers within the crust; and we could check these against what we had learned from the seismic waves of earthquakes gone by. All that and more. A sample of the sediments would give us a complete record of the Earth's history, before man ever made the scene. But there is more involved than that, a lot more.

"Another one?" Martin asked me.

"Yeah. Thanks."

If you study the International Union of Geology and Geophysics publication, *Active Volcanoes of the World,* and if you map out all those which are no longer active, you will note certain volcanic and seismic belts. There is the "Ring of Fire" surrounding the Pacific Ocean. Start along the Pacific coast of South America, and you can follow it up north through Chile, Ecuador, Colombia, Central America, Mexico, the western United States, Canada, and Alaska, then around and down through Kamchatka, the Kuriles, Japan, the Philippines, Indonesia, and New Zealand. Forgetting about the Mediterranean, there is also an area in the Atlantic, near Iceland.

We sat there.

I raised mine and took a sip.

There are over six hundred volcanoes in the world

which could be classified as *active,* though actually they don't do much most of the time.

We were going to add one more.

We were going to create a volcano in the Atlantic Ocean. More specifically, a volcanic island, like Surtsey. This was Project RUMOKO.

"I'm going down again," said Martin. "Sometime during the next few hours, I guess. I'd appreciate it if you would do me the favor of keeping an eye on that goddam machine next time around. I'd make it up to you, some way."

"Okay," I said. "Let me know when the next time is, as soon as you know it, and I'll try to hang around the control room. If something does go wrong, I'll try to do what I did earlier, if there's no one around who can do any better."

He slapped me on the shoulder.

"That's good enough for me. Thanks."

"You're scared."

"Yeah."

"Why?"

"This damned thing seems jinxed. You've been my good-luck charm. I'll buy you beers from here to hell and back again, just to hang around. I don't know what's wrong. Just bad luck, I guess."

"Maybe," I said.

I stared at him for a second, then turned my attention to my drink.

"The isothermic maps show that this is the right place, the right part of the Atlantic," I said. "The only thing I'm sacred about is none of my business."

"What's that?" he asked.

"There are various things about magma," I said, "and some of them frighten me."

"What do you mean?" he asked.

"You don't know what it's going to do, once it's released. It could be anything from a Krakatoa to an Etna.

The magma itself may be of any composition. Its exposure to water and air could produce *any* results."

"I thought we had a guarantee it was safe?"

"A guess. An educated guess, but only a guess. That's all."

"You're scared?"

"You bet your ass."

"We're in danger . . . ?"

"Not *us* so much, since we'll be the hell out of the way. But this thing could affect world temperatures, tides, weather. I'm a little leery, I'll admit it."

He shook his head. "I don't like it."

"You probably had all your bad luck already," I said. "I wouldn't lose any sleep. . . ."

"I guess you're right."

We finished our beers and I stood.

"I've got to be running."

"Can I buy you another?"

"No, thanks. I've got some work to do."

"Well, I'll be seeing you."

"Yes. Take it easy," and I left the lounge and moved back to the upper decks.

The moon spilled sufficient light to make shadows about me, and the evening was chilly enough for me to button my collar.

I watched the waves for a little while, then returned to my cabin.

I took a shower, listened to the late news, read for a time. Finally, I turned in and took the book to bed with me. After a while, I got drowsy, set the book on the bedside table, turned out the lamp, and let the ship rock me to sleep.

. . . Had to get a good night's sleep. After all, tomorrow was RUMOKO.

How long? A few hours, I guess. Then I was awakened by something.

My door was quietly unlocked, and I heard a light footfall.

I lay there, wide awake, with my eyes closed, waiting. I heard the door close, lock.

Then the light came on, and there was a piece of steel near to my head, and a hand was upon my shoulder.

"Wake up, mister!" someone said.

I pretended to do so, slowly.

There were two of them, and I blinked and rubbed my eyes, regarding the gun about twenty inches away from my head.

"What the hell is this?" I said.

"No," said the man holding the metal. "We ask. You answer. It is not the other way around."

I sat up, leaned back against the headboard.

"Okay," I said. "What do you want?"

"Who are you?"

"Albert Schweitzer," I replied.

"We know the name you're using. Who are you—really?"

"That's it," I said.

"We don't think so."

"I'm sorry."

"So are we."

"So?"

"You will tell us about yourself and your mission."

"I don't know what you're talking about."

"Get up!"

"Then please give me my robe. It's hanging on the hook inside the bathroom door."

The gunsel leaned toward the other. "Get it, check it, give it to him," he said.

And I regarded him.

He had a handkerchief over the lower part of his face. So did the other guy. Which was kind of professional. Amateurs tend to wear masks. Upper type. Masks of this sort conceal very little. The lower part of the face is the most easily identifiable.

"Thanks," I said, when the one guy handed me my blue terry-cloth robe.

He nodded, and I threw it about my shoulders, put my arms into the sleeves, whipped it about me, and sat up on the edge of the bed.

"Okay," I said. "What do you want?"

"Who are you working for?" said the first.

"Project RUMOKO," I replied.

He slapped me, lightly, with his left hand, still holding the gun steady.

"No," he said. "The whole story, please."

"I don't know what you're talking about, but may I have a cigarette?"

"All right. —No. Wait. Take one of mine. I don't know what might be in your pack."

I took one, lit it, inhaled, breathed smoke.

"I don't understand you," I said. "Give me a better clue as to what you want to know and maybe I can help you. I'm not looking for trouble."

This seemed to relax them slightly, because they both sighed. The man asking the questions was about five foot eight in height, the other about five-ten. The taller man was heavy, though. Around two hundred pounds, I'd say.

They seated themselves in two nearby chairs. The gun was leveled at my breast.

"Relax, then, Mister Schweitzer. We don't want trouble, either," said the talkative one.

"Great," said I. "Ask me anything and I'll give you honest answers," prepared to lie my head off. "Ask away."

"You repaired the J-9 unit today."

"I guess everybody knows that."

"Why did you do it?"

"Because two men were going to die, and I knew how."

"How did you acquire this expertise?"

"For Chrissakes, I'm an electrical engineer!" I said. "I know how to figure circuits! Lots of people do!"

The taller guy looked at the shorter one. He nodded.

"Then why did you try to silence Asquith?" the taller one asked me.

"Because I broke a regulation by touching the unit," I said. "I'm not authorized to service it."

He nodded again. Both of them had very black and clean-looking hair and well-developed pectorals and biceps, as seen through their light shirts.

"You seem to be an ordinary, honest citizen," said the tall one, "who went to the school of his choice, graduated, remained unmarried, took this job. Perhaps everything is as you say, in which case we do you wrong. However, the circumstances are very suspicious. You repaired a complex machine which you had no right to repair. . . ."

I nodded.

"Why?" he asked.

"I've got a funny thing about death: I don't like to see people do it," I said. Then, "Who do *you* work for?" I asked. "Some sort of intelligence agency?"

The shorter one smiled. The other said, "We are not permitted to say. You obviously understand these things, however. Our interest is only a certain curiosity as to why you kept quiet with respect to what was obviously sabotage."

"So, I've told you."

"Yes, but you are lying. People do not disobey orders the way you did."

"Crap! There were lives at stake!"

He shook his head.

"I fear that we must question you further, and in a different manner."

Whenever I am awaiting the outcome of peril or reflecting upon the few lessons that can be learned in the course of a misspent life, a few bubbles of memory appear before me, are struck by all the color changes the skin of a bubble undergoes in the space of an instant, burst then, having endured no longer than a bubble, and persist as feelings for a long while after.

Bubbles . . . There is one down in the Caribbean called New Eden. Depth, approximately 175 fathoms. As of the most recent census, it was home to over 100,000 people. A huge, illuminated geodesic dome it is, providing an overhead view with which Euclid would have been pleased. For great distances about this dome, strung lights like street lamps line avenues among rocks, bridges over canyons, thoroughfares through mountains. The bottom-going seamobiles move like tanks along these ways; minisubs hover or pass at various altitudes; slick-seeming swimmers in tight and colorful garb come and go, entering and departing the bubble or working about it.

I vacationed there for a couple of weeks one time, and although I discovered claustrophobic tendencies of which I had previously been unaware, it was still quite pleasant. The people were different from surface dwellers. They were rather like what I fancy the old explorers and frontiersmen to have been. Somewhat more individualistic and independent than the average topside citizen, but with a certain sense of community and the feelings of responsibility attendant thereto. This is doubtless because they *are* frontiersmen, having volunteered for combinations of programs involving both the relief of minor population pressures and the exploitation of the ocean's resources. Whatever, they accept tourists. They accepted me, and I went there and swam with them, toured on their subs, viewed their mines and hydroponic gardens, their homes and their public buildings. I remember the beauty of it, I remember the people, I remember the way the sea hung overhead like the night sky as seen through the faceted eye of some insect. Or maybe like a giant insect on the other side, looking in. Yes, that seems more likely. Perhaps the personality of the place appealed to a certain rebellious tendency I occasionally felt stirring fathoms deep within my own psyche.

While it was not really an Eden Under Glass, and

while those crazy and delightful little bubble cities are
definitely not for me, there was something there that
turned it into one of those funny, colorful things that
sometimes come to me, bubblelike, whenever I am
awaiting the outcome of peril or reflecting upon the few
lessons that can be learned in the course of a misspent
life.

I sighed, took a final drag on my cigarette and
crushed it out, knowing that in a moment my bubble
would burst.

What is it like to be the only man in the world who
does not exist? It is difficult to say. It is not easy to gen-
eralize when you are only sure of the particulars in one
case—your own. With me, it was a kind of unusual deal,
and I doubt there is a parallel one, anywhere. I used to
bitch and moan over progressive mechanization. No
more.

It was strange, the way that it happened:

Once I wrote programs for computers. That is how
the whole thing got started.

One day, I learned an unusual and frightening piece
of news . . .

I learned that the whole world was going to exist on
tape.

How?

Well, it's tricky.

Everybody, nowadays, has a birth certificate, academic record, credit rating, a history of all his travels and
places of residence and, ultimately, there is a death certificate somewhere on file. Once, all things of this sort
existed in separate places. Then, some people set out to
combine them. They called it a Central Data Bank. It
resulted in massive changes in the order of human existence. Not all of these changes, I am now certain, were for
the better.

I was one of those people, and it was not until things
were well along that I began to have second thoughts on

the matter. By then, it was too late to do anything about it, I supposed.

What the people in my project were doing was linking every data bank in existence, so that public records, financial records, medical records, specialized technical records all existed and were available from one source —through key stations whose personnel had access to this information at various levels of confidentiality.

I have never considered anything to be wholly good or wholly evil. But this time, I came close to the former feeling. I had thought that it was going to be a very good thing indeed. I had thought that in the wonderful, electrified *fin de siècle* of McLuhan in which we lived, a thing like this was necessary: every home with closed-circuit access to any book ever written, or any play ever recorded on tape or in a crystal, or any college lecture in the past couple of decades, or any bits of general statistical knowledge desired (you can't lie with statistics, theoretically, if everybody has access to your source, and can question it directly); every commercial and government outfit with access to your assets, your income, and a list of every expenditure you've ever made; every attorney with a court order with access to a list of every place you've ever resided, and with whom, and every commercial vehicle on which you've ever traveled, and with whom. Your whole life, all your actions, laid out like a chart of the nervous system in a neurology class—this impressed me as good.

For one thing, it seemed that it would eliminate crime. Only a crazy man, I thought, would care to err with all that to stand against him; and since medical records were all on file, even the psychopath could be stopped.

. . . And speaking of medicine, how fine if the computer and medical people diagnosing you for anything had instant access to all your past medical history! Think of all the cures which could be effected! Think of the deaths prevented!

Think of the status of the world economy, when it is known where every dime exists and where it is headed.

Think of the solving of traffic-control problems—land, sea, and air—when everything is regulated.

Think of . . . Oh, hell!

I foresaw the coming of a Golden Era.

Crap!

A friend of mine having peripheral connections with the Mafia, it was, laughed at me, all starry in my eyes and just up from the university and into the federal service.

"Do you seriously believe that every asset will be registered? Every transaction recorded?" he'd asked me.

"Eventually."

"They haven't pierced Switzerland yet; and if they do, other places will be found."

"There will be a certain allowance for residuals."

"Then don't forget mattresses, and holes in the backyard. Nobody knows how much money there really is in the world, and no one ever will."

So I stopped and thought and read up on economics. He was right. The things for which we were writing programs in this area were, basically, estimates and approximates, vis-à-vis that which got registered—a reconciliation factor included.

So I thought about travel. How many unregistered vessels? Nobody knew. You can't keep statistics on items for which you have no data. And if there is to be unregistered money, more vessels could be constructed. There is a lot of coastline in the world. So traffic control might not be as perfect as I had envisioned.

Medical? Doctors are as human and lazy as the rest of us. I suddenly realized that all medical reports might not get filed—especially if someone wanted to pocket the cash and not pay taxes on it, and was not asked for a receipt.

When it came to people, I had forgotten the human factor.

There were the shady ones, there were people who just liked their privacy, and there were those who would *honestly* foul up the reporting of necessary information. All of them people who would prove that the system was not perfect.

Which meant that the thing might not work in precisely the fashion anticipated. There might also be some resentment, some resistance, along with actual evasion. And perhaps these might even be warranted. . . .

But there was not much overt resistance, so the project proceeded. It occurred over a period of three years. I worked in the central office, starting out as a programmer. After I'd devised a system whereby key weather stations and meteorological observation satellites fed their reports directly into the central system, I was promoted to the position of senior programmer and given some supervisory responsibility.

By then, I had learned sufficient of the project so that my doubts had picked up a few small fears as companions. I found myself beginning to dislike the work, which made me study it all the more intensely. They kidded me about taking work home with me. No one seemed to realize that it was not dedication, but rather a desire, born of my fears, to learn all that I could about the project. Since my superiors misread my actions, they saw that I was promoted once more.

This was fine, because it gave me access to more information, at the policy level. Then, for a variety of reasons, there came a spate of deaths, promotions, resignations, retirements. This left things wide open for fair-haired boys, and I rose higher within the group.

I came to be an adviser to old John Colgate, who was in charge of the entire operation.

One day, when we had just about achieved our mission, I told him of my fears and my doubts. I told the gray-haired, sallow-faced, spaniel-eyed old man that I felt we might be creating a monster and committing the ultimate invasion of human privacy.

He stared at me for a long while, fingering the pink coral paperweight on his desk; then, "You may be right," he said. "What are you going to do about it?"

"I don't know," I replied. "I just wanted to tell you my feelings on the matter."

He sighed then and turned in his swivel chair and stared out the window.

After a time, I thought he had gone to sleep, as he sometimes did right after lunch.

Finally, though, he spoke: "Don't you think I've heard those arguments a thousand times before?"

"Probably," I replied, "and I've always wondered how you might have answered them."

"I have no answers," he said abruptly. "I feel it is for the better, or I would not be associated with it. I could be wrong, though. I will admit that. But some means has to be found to record and regulate all the significant features of a society as complex as ours has become. If you think of a better way of running the show, tell me about it."

I was silent. I lit a cigarette and waited for his next words. I did not know at the time that he only had about six months of life remaining to him.

"Did you ever consider buying out?" he finally asked.

"What do you mean?"

"Resigning. Quitting the system."

"I'm not sure that I understand. . . ."

"We in the system will be the last to have our personal records programmed in."

"Why?"

"Because I wanted it that way, in case anyone came to me as you have today and asked me what you have asked me."

"Has anyone else done it?"

"I would not say if they had, to keep the intended purity of the thing complete."

" 'Buying out.' By this, I take it that you mean destroying my personal data before someone enters it into the system?"

"That is correct," he said.

"But I would not be able to get another job, with no academic record, no past work history . . ."

"That would be your problem."

"I couldn't purchase anything with no credit rating."

"I suppose you would have to pay cash."

"It's all recorded."

He swiveled back and gave me a smile. "Is it?" he asked me. "Is it really?"

"Well, not all of it," I admitted.

"So?"

I thought about it while he lit his pipe, smoke invading wide, white sideburns. Was he just kidding me along, being sarcastic? Or was he serious?

As if in answer to my thought, he rose from his chair, crossed the room, opened a file cabinet. He rummaged around in it for a time, then returned holding a sheaf of punchcards like a poker hand. He dropped them onto the desk in front of me.

"That's you," he said. "Next week, you go into the system, like everybody else," and he puffed a smoke ring and reseated himself.

"Take them home with you and put them under your pillow," he said. "Sleep on them. Decide what you want to do with them."

"I don't understand."

"I am leaving it up to you."

"What if I tore them up? What would you do?"

"Nothing."

"Why not?"

"Because I do not care."

"That's not true. You're head of this thing."

He shrugged.

"Don't you believe in the value of the system yourself?"

He dropped his eyes and drew on his pipe.

"I am no longer so certain as once I was," he stated.

"If I did this thing I would cease to exist, officially," I said.

"Yes."

"What would become of me?"

"That would be your problem."

I thought about it for a moment; then, "Give me the cards," I said.

He did, with a gesture.

I picked them up, placed them in my inside coat pocket.

"What are you going to do now?"

"Sleep on them, as you suggested," I said.

"Just see that you have them back by next Tuesday morning."

"Of course."

And he smiled, nodded, and that was it.

I took them, went home with them. But I didn't sleep. No, that's not it. I wouldn't sleep, couldn't sleep.

I thought about it for centuries—well, all night long —pacing and smoking. To exist outside the system. . . . How could I do anything if it did not recognize my existence?

Then, about four in the morning, I decided that I should have phrased that question the other way around.

How could the system recognize me, no matter what I did?

I sat down then and made some careful plans. In the morning, I tore my cards through the middle, burned them, and stirred the ashes.

"Sit in that chair," the taller one said, gesturing with his left hand.

I did so.

They moved around and stood behind me.

I regulated my breathing and tried to relax.

Over a minute must have gone by; then, "All right, tell us the whole story," he said.

"I obtained this job through a placement bureau," I told him. "I accepted it, came to work, performed my duties, met you. That's it."

"It has been said for some time, and we believe it to be true, that the government can obtain permission—for security reasons—to create a fictitious individual in the central records. An agent is then fitted into that slot in life. If anyone is able to check on him, his credentials appear to be bona fide."

I didn't answer him.

"Is that true?" he asked.

"Yes," I said. "It has been said that this can be done. I don't know whether it's true or not, though."

"You do not admit to being such an agent?"

"No."

Then they whispered to one another for a time. Finally, I heard a metal case click open.

"You are lying."

"No, I'm not. I maybe save a couple guys' lives and you start calling me names. I don't know why, though I'd like to. What have I done that's wrong?"

"I'll ask the questions, Mister Schweitzer."

"I'm just curious. Perhaps if you would tell me—"

"Roll up your sleeve. Either one, it doesn't matter."

"Why?"

"Because I told you to."

"What are you going to do?"

"Administer an injection."

"Are you an M.D.?"

"That is none of your business."

"Well, I refuse it—for the record. After the cops get hold of you, for a variety of reasons, I'll even see to it that the Medical Association is on your back."

"Your sleeve, please."

"Under protest," I observed, and I rolled up the left one. "If you're to kill me when you've finished playing games," I added, "murder is kind of serious. If you are not, I'll be after you. I may find you one day. . . ."

I felt a sting behind my biceps.

"Mind telling me what you gave me?" I asked.

"It's called TC-6," he replied. "Perhaps you've read about it. You will retain consciousness, as I might need your full reasoning abilities. But you will answer me honestly."

I chuckled, which they doubtless attributed to the effects of the drug, and I continued practicing my yoga breathing techniques. These could not stop the drug, but they made me feel better. Maybe they gave me a few extra seconds, also, along with the detached feeling I had been building up.

I keep up on things like TC-6. This one, I knew, left you rational, unable to lie, and somewhat literal-minded. I figured on making the most of its weak points by flowing with the current. Also, I had a final trick remaining.

The thing that I disliked most about TC-6 was that it sometimes had a bad side effect, cardiac-wise.

I did not exactly feel myself going under. I was just suddenly there, and it did not feel that different from the way I always feel. I knew that to be an illusion. I wished I had had prior access to the antidote kit I kept within a standard-looking first-aid kit hidden in my dresser.

"You hear me, don't you?" he asked.

"Yes," I heard myself saying.

"What is your name?"

"Albert Schweitzer," I replied.

There were a couple of quick breaths taken behind me, and my questioner silenced the other fellow, who had started to say something.

Then, "What do you do?" he asked me.

"I'm a technician."

"I know that much. What else?"

"I do many things—"

"Do you work for the government—*any* government?"

"I pay taxes, which means I work for the government, part of the time. Yes."

"I did not mean it in that sense. Are you a secret agent in the employ of any government?"

"No."

"A *known* agent?"

"No."

"Then why are you here?"

"I am a technician. I service the machines."

"What else?"

"I do not—"

"What else? Who else do you work for, besides the Project?"

"Myself."

"What do you mean?"

"My activities are directed to maintaining my personal economic status and physical well-being."

"I am talking about other employers. Have you any?"

"No."

From the other man, I heard, "He sounds clean."

"Maybe." Then, to me, "What would you do if you met me somewhere and recognized me?"

"Bring you to law."

". . . And failing that?"

"If I were able, I would hurt you severely. Perhaps I would kill you, if I were able to give it the appearance of self-defense or make it seem to be an accident."

"Why?"

"Because I wish to preserve my own physical well-being. The fact that you had disturbed it once means that you might attempt it again. I will not permit this access to me."

"I doubt that I will attempt it again."

"Your doubts mean nothing to me."

"So you saved two lives today, yet you are willing to take one."

I did not reply.

"Answer me."

"You did not ask me a question."

"Could he have drug-consciousness?" asked the other.

"I never thought of that. —Do you?"

"I do not understand the question."

"This drug allows you to remain oriented in all three spheres. You know who you are, where you are, and when you are. It saps that thing called the will, however, which is why you must answer my questions. A person with a lot of experience with truth drugs can sometimes beat them, by rephrasing the questions to himself and giving a literally honest reply. Is this what you are doing?"

"That's the wrong question," said the other.

"What's right?"

"Have you had any prior experience with drugs?" that one asked me.

"Yes."

"What ones?"

"I've had aspirin, nicotine, caffeine, alcohol—"

"Truth serums," he said. "Things like this, things that make you talk. Have you had them before?"

"Yes."

"Where?"

"At Northwestern University."

"Why?"

"I volunteered for a series of experiments."

"What did they involve?"

"The effects of drugs on consciousness."

"Mental reservations," he said to the other. "It could take days. I think he has primed himself."

"Can you beat a truth drug?" the other one asked me.

"I do not understand."

"Can you lie to us—now?"

"No."

"Wrong question, again," said the shorter. "He is not lying. Anything he says is literally true."

"So how do we get an answer out of him?"

"I'm not sure."

So they continued to hit me with questions. After a time, things began to wane.

"He's got us," said the shorter one. "It would take days to beat him down."

"Should we . . . ?"

"No. We've got the tape. We've got his answers. Let's let a computer worry about it."

But by then it was near morning, and I had the funny feeling, accompanied by cold flashes on the back of my neck, that I might be able to manage a fib or three once again. There was some light on the other side of my portholes. They had been going at me for what seemed to be many hours. I decided to try.

"I think this place is bugged," I said.

"What? What do you mean?"

"Ship's Security," I stated. "I believe all technicians are so monitored."

"Where is it?"

"I don't know."

"We've got to find it," said the one.

"What good will it do?" said the other, in a whisper, for which I respected him, as whispers do not often get recorded. "They'd have been here long before this, if it were."

"Unless they're waiting, letting us hang ourselves."

The first began looking, however, and I rose, met with no objections, and staggered across the room to collapse upon the bed.

My right hand slipped down around the headboard, as though by accident. It found the gun.

I flipped off the safety as I withdrew it. I sat upon the bed and pointed it at them.

"All right, morons," I said. "Now you answer *my* questions."

The big one made a move toward his belt and I shot him in the shoulder.

"Next?" I asked, tearing away the silencer, which had done its work, and replacing it with a pillow.

The other man raised his hands and looked at his buddy.

"Let him bleed," I said.

"He nodded and stepped back.

"Sit down," I told them both.

They did.

I moved over behind the two of them.

"Give me that arm," and I took it. I cleaned it and dressed it, as the bullet had gone on through. I had placed their weapons on the dresser. I tore off their hankies and studied their faces. I did not know them from anywhere.

"Okay, why are you here?" I asked. "And why do you want to know what you want to know?"

There were no replies.

"I don't have as much time as you did," I said. "So I'm about to tape you in place. I don't think I can afford to fool around with drugs."

I fetched the adhesive tape from the medicine chest and did it.

"These places are pretty soundproof," I remarked, putting the gun aside, "and I lied about them being bugged. —So you can do a bit of screaming if you want. I caution you against it, however. Each one earns you one broken bone.

"So who do *you* work for?" I repeated.

"I'm a maintenance man on the shuttler," said the shorter one. "My friend is a pilot."

He received a dirty look for this.

"Okay," I said. "I'll buy that, because I've never seen you around here before. Think carefully over your answer to the next one: who do you *really* work for?"

I asked this knowing that they did not have the advantages that I had had. I work for myself because I am self-employed—an independent contractor. My name is Albert Schweitzer right now, so that's what it is, period.

I always become the person I must. Had they asked me who I had been before, they might have gotten a different answer. It's a matter of conditioning and mental attitudes.

"Who pulls the strings?" I asked.

No replies.

"All right," I said. "I guess I'll have to ask you in a different fashion."

Heads turned toward me.

"You were willing to violate my physiology for the sake of a few answers," I said. "Okay. I guess I'll return the favor upon your anatomy. I'll get an answer or three, I promise. Only I'll be a little more basic about it. I'll simply torture you until you talk."

"You wouldn't do that," said the taller man. "You have a low violence index."

I chuckled.

"Let's see," I said.

How do you go about ceasing to exist while continuing your existence? I found it quite easy. But then, I was in on the project from the first, was trusted, had been given an option . . .

After I tore up my cards, I returned to work as usual. There, I sought and located the necessary input point. That was my last day on the job.

It was Thule, way up where it's cold, a weather station. . . .

An old guy who liked rum ran the place. I can still remember the day when I took my ship, the *Proteus,* into his harbor and complained of rough seas.

"I'll put you up," he said to me.

The computer had not let me down.

"Thanks."

He led me in, fed me, talked to me about the seas, the weather. I brought in a case of Bacardi and turned him loose on it.

"Ain't things pretty much automatic here?" I asked.

"That's right."

"Then what do they need you for?"

He laughed a little and said, "My uncle was a Senator. I needed a place to go. He fixed me up. —Let's see your ship. —So what's if it's raining?"

So we did.

It was a decent-sized cabin cruiser with powerful engines—and way out of its territory.

"It's a bet," I told him. "I wanted to hit the Arctic Circle and get proof that I did."

"Kid, you're nuts."

"I know, but I'll win."

"Prob'ly," he agreed. "I was like you once—all full of the necessary ingredients and ready to go. —Gettin' much action these days?" And he stroked his pepper-and-salt beard and gave me an evil grin from inside it.

"Enough," I said, and, "Have a drink," because he had made me think of Eva.

He did, and I left it at, "Enough," for a time. She was not like that, though. I mean, it was not something he would really want to hear about.

It had been about four months earlier that we had broken up. It was not religion or politics; it was much more basic.

So I lied to him about an imaginary girl and made him happy.

I had met her in New York, back when I was doing the same things she was—vacationing and seeing plays and pix.

She was a tall girl, with close-cropped blond hair. I helped her find a subway station, got on with her, got off with her, asked her to dinner, was told to go to hell.

Scene:

"I'm not like that."

"Neither am I. But I'm hungry. —So *will* you?"

"What are you looking for?"

"Someone to talk to," I said. "I'm lonesome."

"I think you're looking in the wrong place."

"Probably."

"I don't know you from anywhere."

"That makes two of us, but I could sure use some spaghetti with meat sauce and a glass of Chianti."

"Will you be hard to get rid of?"

"No. I go quietly."

"Okay. I'll eat spaghetti with you."

And we did.

That month we kept getting closer and closer until we were there. The fact that she lived in one of those crazy little bubble cities under the sea meant nothing. I was liberal enough to appreciate the fact that the Sierra Club had known what it was doing in pushing for their construction.

I probably should have gone along with her when she went back. She had asked me.

She had been on vacation—seeing the Big Place—and so had I. I didn't get into New York that often.

"Marry me," though, I'd said.

But she would not give up her bubble and I would not give up my dream. I wanted the big, above-the-waves world—all of it. I loved that blue-eyed bitch from five hundred fathoms, though, and I realize now that I probably should have taken her on her own terms. I'm too damned independent. If either of us had been normal . . . Well, we weren't, and that's that.

Eva, wherever you are, I hope you and Jim are happy.

"Yeah—with Coke," I said. "It's good that way," and I drank Cokes and he drank doubles with Cokes until he announced his weariness.

"It's starting to get to me, Mister Hemingway," he said.

"Well, let's sack out."

"Okay. You can have the couch there."

"Great."

"I showed you where the blankets are?"

"Yes."

"Then good night, Ernie. See you in the morning."

"You bet, Bill. I'll make breakfast for us."

"Thanks."

And he yawned and stretched and went away.

I gave him half an hour and went to work.

His weather station had a direct line into the central computer. I was able to provide for a nice little cut-in. Actuated by short wave. Little-used band. I concealed my tamperings well.

When I was finished, I knew that I had it made.

I could tell Central anything through that thing, from hundreds of miles away, and it would take it as fact.

I was damn near a god.

Eva, maybe I should have gone the other way. I'll never know.

I helped Bill Mellings over his hangover the following morning, and he didn't suspect a thing. He was a very decent old guy, and I was comforted by the fact that he would never get into trouble over what I had done. This was because nobody would ever catch me, I was sure. And even if they do, I don't think he'll get into trouble. After all, his uncle was a Senator.

I had the ability to make it as anybody I cared to. I'd have to whip up the entire past history—birth, name, academics, and *et cet*—and I could then fit myself in anywhere I wanted in modern society. All I had to do was tell Central via the weather station via short wave. The record would be created and I would have existence in any incarnation I desired. *Ab initio*, like.

But Eva, I wanted you. I— Well . . .

I think the government does occasionally play the same tricks. But I am positive they don't suspect the existence of an independent contractor.

I know most of that which is worth knowing—more than is necessary, in fact—with respect to lie detectors and truth serums. I hold my name sacred. Nobody gets it. Do you know that the polygraph can be beaten in no fewer than seventeen different ways? It has not been much improved since the mid-twentieth century. A lower-chest strap plus some fingertip perspiration detectors could do it wonders. But things like this never get the appropriations. Maybe a few universities play around with it from this standpoint—but that's about it. I could design one today that damn near nobody could beat, but its record still wouldn't be worth much in court. Drugs, now, they're another matter.

A pathological liar can beat Amytal and Pentothal. So can a drug-conscious guy.

What is drug-consciousness?

Ever go looking for a job and get an intelligence test or an aptitude test or a personality inventory for your pains? Sure. Everybody has by now, and they're all on file in Central. You get used to taking them after a time. They start you in early, and throughout your life you learn about taking the goddamn things. You get to be what psychologists refer to as "test-conscious." What it means is that you get so damned used to them that you know what kind of asininity is right, according to the book.

So okay. You learn to give them the answers they're looking for. You learn all the little time-saving tricks. You feel secure, you know it is a game and you are game-conscious.

It's the same thing.

If you do not get scared, and if you have tried a few drugs before for this express purpose, you can beat them.

Drug-consciousness is nothing more than knowing how to handle yourself under that particular kind of fire.

"Go to hell. You answer my questions," I said.

I think that the old tried-and-true method of getting answers is the best: pain, threatened and actual.

I used it.

I got up early in the morning and made breakfast. I took him a glass of orange juice and shook him by the shoulder.

"What the goddam—!"

"Breakfast," I said. "Drink this."

He did, and then we went out to the kitchen and ate.

"The sea looks pretty good today," I said. "I guess I can be moving on."

He nodded above his eggs.

"You ever up this way, you stop in again. Hear?"

"I will," I said, and I have—several times since—because I came to like him. It was funny.

We talked all that morning, going through three pots of coffee. He was an M.D. who had once had a fairly large practice going for him. (At a later date, he dug a few bullets out of me and kept quiet about their having been there.) He had also been one of the early astronauts, briefly. I learned subsequently that his wife had died of cancer some six years earlier. He gave up his practice at that time, and he did not remarry. He had looked for a way to retire from the world, found one, done it.

Though we are very close friends now, I have never told him that he's harboring a bastard input unit. I may, one day, as I know he is one of the few guys I can trust. On the other hand, I do not want to make him a genuine accomplice to what I do. Why trouble your friends and make them morally liable for your strange doings?

So I became the man who did not exist. But I had acquired the potential for becoming anybody I chose. All I had to do was write the program and feed it to Central via that station. All I needed then was a means of living. This latter was a bit tricky.

I wanted an occupation where payment would always be made to me in cash. Also, I wanted one where payment would be large enough for me to live as I desired.

This narrowed the field considerably and threw out lots of legitimate things. I could provide myself with a conventional-seeming background in any area that amused me, and work as an employee there. Why should I, though?

I created a new personality and moved into it. Those little things you always toy with and dismiss as frivolous whims—I did them then. I lived aboard the *Proteus,* which at that time was anchored in the cove of a small island off the New Jersey coast.

I studied judo. There are three schools of it, you know: there is the Kodokon, or the pure Japanese style, and there are the Budo Kwai and the French Federation systems. The latter two have pretty much adopted the rules of the former, with this exception: while they use the same chokes, throws, bone-locks, and such, they're sloppier about it. They feel that the pure style was designed to accommodate the needs of a smaller race, with reliance upon speed, leverage, and agility, rather than strength. So they attempted to adapt the basic techniques to the needs of a larger race. They allowed for the use of strength and let the techniques be a little less than perfect. This was fine so far as I was concerned, because I'm a big, sloppy guy. Only, I may be haunted one day because of my laxity. If you learn it the Kodokon way, you can be eighty years old and still carry off a *nage-no-kata* perfectly. This is because there is very little effort involved; it's all technique. My way, though, when you start pushing fifty, it gets rougher and rougher because you're not as strong as you once were. Well, that still gave me a couple of decades in which to refine my form. Maybe I'll make it. I made *Nidan* with the French Federation, so I'm not a complete slouch. And I try to stay in shape.

While I was going for all this physical activity I took a locksmith course. It took me weeks to learn to pick even the simplest lock, and I still think that the most efficient way, in a pinch, is to break the door in, get what you want, and run like hell.

I was not cut out to be a criminal, I guess. Some guys have it and some don't.

I studied every little thing I could think of that I thought would help me get by. I still do. While I am probably not an expert in anything, except perhaps for my own peculiar mode of existence, I know a little bit about lots of esoteric things. And I have the advantage of not existing going for me.

When I ran low on cash, I went to see Don Walsh. I knew who he was, although he knew nothing about me, and I hoped that he never would. I'd chosen him as my modus vivendi.

That was over ten years ago, and I still can't complain. Maybe I am even a little better with the locks and nages these days, as a result thereof—not to mention the drugs and bugs.

Anyhow, that is a part of it, and I send Don a card every Christmas.

I couldn't tell whether they thought I was bluffing. They had said I had a low violence index, which meant they had had access to my personnel file or to Central. Which meant I had to try keeping them off balance for the time I had remaining, there on the Eve of RUMO-KO. But my bedside alarm showed five till six, and I went on duty at eight o'clock. If they knew as much as they seemed to know, they probably had access to the duty rosters also.

So here was the break I had spent the entire month seeking, right in the palm of my hand on the Eve of RUMOKO's rumble. Only, if they knew how much time I actually had in which to work them over, they might —probably could—be able to hold out on me. I was not about to leave them in my cabin all day; and the only alternative was to turn them over to Ship's Security before I reported for duty. I was loath to do this, as I did not know whether there were any others aboard—whoever they were—or if they had anything more planned, since the J-9 trouble had not come off as they had expected. Had it succeeded, it would surely have postponed the September 15 target date.

I had a fee to earn, which meant I had a package to deliver. The box was pretty empty, so far.

"Gentlemen," I said, my voice sounding strange to me and my reflexes seeming slow. I therefore attempted to restrict my movements as much as possible, and to speak slowly and carefully. "Gentlemen, you've had your turn. Now it is mine." I turned a chair backward and seated myself upon it, resting my gun hand on my forearm and my forearm on the back of the chair. "I will, however," I continued, "preface my actions with that which I have surmised concerning yourselves.

"You are *not* government agents," I said, glancing from one to the other. "No. You represent a private interest of some sort. If you are agents, you should doubtless have been able to ascertain that I am not one. You resorted to the extreme of questioning me in this fashion, however, so my guess is that you are civilians and perhaps somewhat desperate at this point. This leads me to link you with the attempted sabotage of the J-9 unit this previous afternoon. —Yes, let's call it sabotage. You know that it was, and you know that I know it—since I worked on the thing and it didn't come off as planned. This obviously prompted your actions of this evening. Therefore, I shan't even ask you the question.

"Next, and predicated upon my first assumption, I know that your credentials are genuine. I could fetch them from your pockets in a moment, if they are there, but your names would mean nothing to me. So I will not even go looking. There is really only one question that I want answered, and it probably won't even hurt your employer or employers, who will doubtless disavow any knowledge of you.

"I want to know who you represent," I said.

"Why?" asked the larger man, his frown revealing a lip-side scar which I had not noticed at his unmasking.

"I want to know who put you up to being so casual with my person," I said.

"To what end?"

I shrugged.

"Personal vengeance, perhaps."

He shook his head.

"You're working for somebody, too," he said. "If it is not the government, it is still somebody we wouldn't like."

"So you admit you are not independent operators. If you will not tell me who you work for, will you tell me why you want to stop the project?"

"No."

"All right. Drop that one. —I see you as associated with some large contractor who got cut out on something connected with this job. How does that sound? Maybe I can even make suggestions."

The other guy laughed, and the big one killed it with a quick glare.

"Well, that's out," I said. "Thanks. Now, let's consider another thing: I can simply turn you in for breaking and entering. I might even be willing to say you were drunk and indicated that you thought this cabin belonged to a friend of yours who didn't mind a little foolery and who you thought might stand you to a final round before you staggered off to bed. How does that sound?"

"*Is* this place bugged, or isn't it?" asked the shorter one, who seemed a bit younger than the other.

"Of course not," said his partner. "Just keep your mouth shut."

"Well, how does it sound?" I asked.

He shook his head again.

"Well, the alternative is my telling the whole story, drugs, questions, and all. How does *that* sound? How will you stand up under protracted questioning?"

The big one thought about it, shook his head again.

"*Will* you?" he finally asked me.

"Yes, I will."

He seemed to consider this.

". . . Then," I concluded, "I cannot save you the pain, as I wish to. Even if you possess drug-consciousness, you know that you will break within a couple of days if they use drugs as well as all the other tricks. It is simply a matter of talking now or talking later. Since you prefer to defer it, I can only assume that you have something else planned to stop RUMOKO—"

"He's too damned smart!"

"Tell him to shut up again," I said. "He's giving me my answers too fast and depriving me of my fun. —So what is it? Come on," I said. "I'll get it, one way or another, you know."

"He is right," said the man with the scar. "You *are* too damned smart. Your I.Q. and your Personality Profile show nothing like this. Would you be open to an offer?"

"Maybe," I said. "But it would have to be a big one. Give me the terms, and tell me who's offering."

"Terms: a quarter of a million dollars, cash," he said, "and that is the maximum I can offer. Turn us loose and go about your business. Forget about tonight."

I *did* think about it. Let's face it, it was tempting. But I go through a lot of money in a few years' time, and I hated to report failure to Walsh's Private Investigations, the third-largest detective agency in the world, with whom I wished to continue associating myself, as an independent contractor.

"So who foots the bill? How? And why?"

"I can get you half that amount tonight, in cash, and the other half in a week to ten days. You tell us how you want it, and that is the way it will be. 'Why?' though, do not ask that question. It will be one of the things we will be buying."

"Your boss obviously has a lot of money to throw around," I said, glancing at the clock and seeing that it was now six fifteen. "No, I must refuse your offer."

"Then you could not be a government man. One of them would take it, and then make an arrest."

"I already told you that. So what else is new?"

"We seem to have reached an impasse, Mister Schweitzer."

"Hardly," I replied. "We have simply reached the end of my preface. Since reasoning with you has failed, I must now take positive action. I apologize for this, but it is necessary."

"You are really going to resort to physical violence?"

"I'm afraid so," I said. "And don't worry. I expected a hangover this morning, so I signed for sick leave last night. I have all day. You already have a painful flesh wound, so I'll give you a break this time around."

Then I stood, cautiously, and the room swayed, but I did not let it show. I crossed to the smaller guy's chair and seized its arms and his together and raised them up from off the floor. Woozy, I was; but not weak.

I carried him off to the bathroom and set him, chair and all, in the shower stall, avoiding the while many forward thrustings of his head.

Then I returned to the other.

"Just to keep you abreast of what is going on," I said, "it all depends on the time of day. I have measured the temperature of the hot water in that stall at various times, and it can come out of there at anything from 140° to 180° Fahrenheit. Your buddy is about to get it, hot and full blast, as soon as I open his shirt and trousers and expose as much bare flesh as possible. You understand?"

"I understand."

I went back inside and opened him up and turned the shower on, using the hot water only. Then I went back to the main room. I studied the features of his buddy, who I then noted bore him something of a resemblance. It struck me that they might be relatives.

When the screaming began, he sought to compose his features. But I could see I was getting through to him.

He tested his restraints once again, looked at my clock, looked at me.

"Turn it off, God damn you!" he cried.

"Your cousin?" I asked him.

"My half brother! Shut it down, you baboon!"

"Only if you've got something to say to me."

"Okay! But leave him in there and close the door!"

I dashed and did it. My head was beginning to clear, though I still felt like hell.

I burned my right hand shutting the thing down. I left my chosen victim slouched there in the steam, and I shut the door behind me as I returned to the main room.

"What do you have to say?"

"Could you give me one free hand and a cigarette?"

"No, but you can have a cigarette."

"How about the right one? I can hardly move it."

I considered, and said, "Okay," picking up my gun again.

I lit the stick, stuck it in his mouth, then cut the tape and tore it off his right forearm. He dropped the cigarette when I did it, and I picked it up and restored it to him.

"All right," I said, "take ten seconds and enjoy yourself. After that, we talk cases."

He nodded, looked around the room, took a deep drag, and exhaled.

"I guess you *do* know how to hurt," he said. "If you are not government, I guess your file is very much off."

"I am not government."

"Then I wish you were on our side, because it is a pretty bad thing. Whatever you are, or do," he stated, "I hope you are aware of the full implications."

. . . And he glanced at my clock, again.

Six twenty-five.

He had done it several times, and I had dismissed it. But now it seemed something more than a desire to know the time.

"When does it go off?" I asked, on chance.

Buying that, on chance, he replied, "Bring my brother back, where I can see him."

"When does it go off?" I repeated.

"Too soon," he replied, "and then it will not matter. You are too late."

"I don't think so," I said. "But now that I know, I'll have to move, fast. So . . . Don't lose any sleep over it. I think I am going to turn you in now."

"What if I could offer you more money?"

"Don't. You'd only embarrass me. And I'd still say, 'No.' "

"Okay. But bring him back, please—and take care of his burns."

So I did.

"You guys will remain here for a brief while," I finally said, snuffing the older one's cigarette and retaping his wrist. Then I moved toward the door.

"You don't know, you really don't know!" I heard from behind me.

"Don't fool yourself," I said, over my shoulder.

I didn't know. I really didn't know.

But I could guess.

I stormed through the corridors until I reached Carol Deith's cabin. There I banged upon the door until I heard some muffled cursing and a "Wait a minute!" Then the door opened and she stared out at me, her eyes winking at the light, a slumber cap of sorts upon her head and a bulky robe about her.

"What do you want?" she asked me.

"Today is the day indeed," I said. "I've got to talk to you. May I come in?"

"No," she said. "I'm not accustomed to—"

"Sabotage," I said. "I know. That's what it's all about, and it isn't finished yet. —Please . . ."

"Come in." The door was suddenly wide open and she was standing to one side.

I entered.

She closed the door behind me, leaned back against it and said, "All right, what is it?"

There was a feeble light glowing, and a messed-up bed from which I had obviously aroused her.

"Look, maybe I didn't give you the whole story the other day," I told her. "*Yes,* it was sabotage—and there was a bomb, and I disposed of it. That's over and done with. Today is the big day, though, and the final attempt is in the offing. I know that for a fact. I think I know what it is and where it is. Can you help me? Can I help you? Help."

"Sit down," she said.

"There isn't much time."

"Sit down, please. I have to get dressed."

"Please hurry."

She stepped into the next room and left the door open. I was around the corner from it, though, so it should not have bothered her if she trusted me—and I guess she did, because she did.

"What is it?" she asked me, amidst the rustle of clothing.

"I believe that one or more of our three atomic charges has been booby-trapped, so that the bird will sing a bit prematurely within its cage."

"Why?" she said.

"Because there are two men back in my cabin, both of them taped to chairs, who tried to make me talk earlier this evening, with respect to my servicing of the J-9."

"What does that prove?"

"They were kind of rough on me."

"So?"

"When I got the upper hand, I got the same way with them. I made them talk."

"How?"

"None of your business. But they talked. I think RU-MOKO's ignitors need another check."

"I can pick them up in your cabin?"

"Yes."

"How did you apprehend them?"

"They didn't know I had a gun."

"I see. Neither did I. —We'll get them, don't worry. But you are telling me that you took both of them and beat some answers out of them?"

"More or less," I said, "and yes and no, and off the record—in case this place is bugged. Is it?"

She came in, nodded her head and put a finger to her lips.

"Well, let's go do something," I said. "We'd better act quickly, I don't want these guys fouling the project all up."

"They won't. Okay. I'll give it to you that you know what you are doing. I will take you at face value as a strange creature. You did something which nobody expected of you. This does happen occasionally. We sometimes meet up with a guy who knows his job thoroughly and can see when something is going wrong—and who cares enough about it to proceed from there and damn the torpedoes. You say an atomic bomb will soon be going off aboard this ship. Right?"

"Yes."

"You think one of the charges has been attached, and has a timer cued in?"

"Right," and I looked at my wristwatch and saw that it was going on seven.

"I'd bet less than an hour from now."

"They're going down in a few minutes," she told me.

"What are you going to do about it?"

She picked up the telephone on the little table next to her bed.

"Operations," she said. "Stop the countdown." Then, "Give me the barracks. "Sergeant," she then said, "I want you to make some arrests." She looked at me. "What is your room number?" she asked.

"Six-forty," I replied.

"Six-forty," she said. "Two men. —Right. —Yes. —Thank you." And she hung up.

"They're taken care of," she told me. "So, you think a charge might go off prematurely?"

"That's what I said—twice."

"Could you stop it?"

"With the proper equipment—though I'd rather you send in a service—"

"Get it," she said to me.

"Okay," and I went and did that thing.

I came back to her cabin around five minutes later, with a heavy pack slung over my shoulder.

"I had to sign my name in blood," I told her. "But I've got what I need. —Why don't you get yourself a good physicist?"

"I want you," she said. "You were in from the beginning. You know what you're doing. Let's keep the group small and tight."

"Tell me where to go to do it," I said, and she led the way.

It was pushing seven by then.

It took me ten minutes to find out which one they had done it to.

It was child's play. They had used the motor from an advanced kid's erector set—with self-contained power unit. It was to be actuated by a standard clock-type timer, which would cause it to pull the lead shielding. The damned thing would go off while it was on the way down.

It took me less than ten minutes to disarm it.

We stood near the railing, and I leaned upon it.

"Good," I said.

"Very good," she said.

"While you're at it," she continued, "get on your guard. You are about to be the subject of the biggest security investigation I have ever set off."

"Go ahead. I'm pure as snow and swansdown."

"You aren't real," she told me. "They don't make people like that."

"So touch me," I said. "I am sorry if you don't like the way I go about existing."

"If you don't turn into a frog come midnight, a girl could learn to like a guy like you."

"That would require a very stupid girl," I said.

And she gave me a strange look which I did not really care to try interpreting.

Then she stared me straight in the eyes.

"You've got some kind of secret I do not quite understand yet," she said. "You seem like a leftover from the Old Days."

"Maybe I am. Look, you've already said that I've been of help. Why not leave it at that? I haven't done anything wrong."

"I've got a job to do. But, on the other hand, you're right. You have helped, and you haven't really broken any regs. —Except with reference to the J-9, for which I'm sure nobody is going to cause you trouble. On the opposite hand, I've got a report to write. Of necessity, your actions will figure in it prominently. I can't very well leave you out."

"I wasn't asking that," I said.

"What do you want me to do?"

Once it got into Central, I knew, I could kill it. But prior to that, it would be filtered through a mess of humans. They could cause trouble. "You kept the group small and tight," I said. "You could drop one."

"No."

"Okay. I could be a draftee, from the beginning."

"That's better."

"Then maybe we could let it be that way."

"I see no great problems."

"You'll do it?"

"I will see what I can do."

"That's enough. Thanks."

"What will you do when your job here is finished?"

"I don't know. Take a vacation, maybe."

"All alone?"

"Maybe."

"Look, I like you. I'll do things to keep you out of trouble."

"I'd appreciate that."

"You seem to have answers for everything."

"Thank you."

"What about a girl?"

"What do you mean?"

"Could you use one, in whatever you do?"

"I thought you had a pretty good job here."

"I do. That's not what I'm talking about. —Do you have one?"

"One what?"

"Stop playing the stupid role. —A girl, is what I mean."

"No."

"Well?"

"You're nuts," I said. "What the hell could I do with an Intelligence-type girl? Do you mean that you would actually take the chance of teaming up with a stranger?"

"I've watched you in action, and I'm not afraid of you. Yes, I would take the chance."

"This is the strangest proposal I've ever received."

"Think quick," she said.

"You don't know what you're asking," I told her.

"What if I like you—an awful lot?"

"Well, I disarmed your bomb. . . ."

"I'm not talking about being grateful. —But thanks, anyway. —The answer, I take it, is, 'No.'"

"Stop that! Can't you give a man a chance to think?"

"Okay," she said, and turned away.

"Wait. Don't be that way. You can't hurt me, so I can talk honestly. I *do* have a crush on you. I have been a confirmed bachelor for many years, though. You are a complication."

"Let's look at it this way," she told me. "You're different, I know that. I wish *I* could do different things."

"Like what?"

"Lie to computers and get away with it."

"What makes you say that?"

"It's the only answer, if you're real."

"I'm real."

"Then you know how to beat the system."

"I doubt it."

"Take me along," she said. "I'd like to do the same thing."

And I looked at her. A little wisp of hair was touching her cheek, and she looked as if she wanted to cry.

"I'm your last chance, aren't I? You met me at a strange moment in your life, and you want to gamble."

"Yes."

"You're nuts, and I can't promise you security unless you want to quit the game—and *I* can't. I play it by my own rules, though—and they're kind of strange. If you and I got together, you would probably be a young widow. —So you would have *that* going for you."

"You're tough enough to disarm bombs."

"I will meet an early grave. I do lots of stupid things when I have to."

"I think I might be in love with you."

"Then, for gods' sakes, let me talk to you later. I have lots of things to think about, now."

"All right."

"You're a dumb broad."

"I don't think so."

"Well, we'll see."

After I woke up from one of the deepest sleeps in my life, I went and signed for duty.

"You're late," said Morrey.

"So have them dock me."

I went then and watched the thing itself begin to occur.

RUMOKO was in the works.

They went down, Martin and Demmy, and planted the charge. They did the necessary things, and we got out of there. Everything was set, and waiting for our radio signal. My cabin had been emptied of intruders, and I was grateful.

We got far enough away, and the signal was given.

All was silent for a time. Then the bomb went off.

Over the port bow, I saw the man stand up. He was old and gray and wore a wide-brimmed hat. He stood, slouched, fell on his face.

"We've just polluted the atmosphere some more," said Martin.

"Hell," said Demmy.

The oceans rose and assailed us. The ship held anchor.

For a time, there was nothing. Then, it began.

The ship shook, like a wet dog. I clung to the rail and watched. Next came a mess of waves, and they were bastards, but we rode them out.

"We've got the first reading," said Carol. "It's beginning to build."

I nodded and did not say anything. There wasn't much to say.

"It's getting bigger," she said, after a minute, and I nodded again.

Finally, later on that morning, the whole thing that had come loose made its scene upon the surface.

The waters had been bubbling for a long while by then. The bubbles grew larger. The temperature readings rose. There came a glow.

Then there was one fantastic spout. It was blasted into the air to a great height, golden in the morning sunshine, like Zeus when he had visited one of his girlfriends or other. It was accompanied by a loud roar. It hung there for a few brief moments, then descended in a shower of sparks.

Immediately thereafter, there was greater turbulence.

It increased and I watched, the regular way and by means of the instruments.

The waters frothed and glistened. The roaring came and went. There came another spout, and another. The waters burned beneath the waves. Four more spouts, each larger than its predecessor. . . .

Then an ocean-riving blast caught the *Aquina* in something close to a tidal wave. . . .

We were ready, though—built that way—and faced into it.

We rode with it, and there was no letup.

We were miles away, and it seemed as if but an arm's distance separated us.

The next spout just kept going up, until it became a topless pillar. It pierced the sky, and a certain darkness began at that point. It began to swell, and there were fires all about its base.

After a time, the entire sky was fading over into a false twilight, and a fine dust filled the air, the eyes, the lungs. Occasionally, a crowd of ashes passed in the distance, like a covey of dark birds. I lit a cigarette to protect my lungs against pollution, and watched the fires rise.

With our early evening, the seas darkened. The kraken himself, disturbed, might have been licking our hull. The glow continued, and a dark form appeared.

RUMOKO.

It was the cone. An artificially created island. A piece of long-sunk Atlantis itself, perhaps, was rising in the distance. Man had succeeded in creating a landmass. One day it would be habitable. Now, if we made a chain of them . . .

Yes. Perhaps another Japan. More room for the expanding human race. More space. More places in which to live.

Why had I been questioned? Who had opposed this? It was a good thing, as I saw it.

I went away. I went and had dinner.

Carol came into the commissary and joined me, as if by accident. I nodded, and she seated herself across from me and ordered.

"Hi."

"Hi."

"Maybe you've done some of your thinking by now?" she said, between the salad and the ersatz beef.

"Yes," I replied.

"What are the results?"

"I still don't know. It was awfully quick and, frankly, I'd like the opportunity to get to know you a little better."

"Signifying what?"

"There is an ancient custom known as 'dating.' Let's do it for a little while."

"You don't like me? I've checked our compatibility indices. They show that we would be okay together—buying you at face value, that is—but I think I know more of you than that."

"Outside of the fact that I'm not for sale, what does that mean?"

"I've made lots of guesses and I think I could also get along with an individualist who knows how to play the right games with machines."

I knew that the commissary was bugged, and I guessed that she didn't know that I did. Therefore, she had a reason for saying what she had said—and she didn't think I knew about it.

"Sorry. Too quick," I told her. "Give a man a chance, will you?"

"Why don't we go someplace and discuss it?"

We were ready for dessert at that point.

"Where?"

"Spitzbergen."

I thought about it, then, "Okay," I said.

"I'll be ready in about an hour and a half."

"Whoa!" I said. "I thought you meant, like—perhaps

this weekend. There are still tests to run, and I'm scheduled for duty."

"But your job here is finished, isn't it?"

I started in on my dessert—apple pie, and pretty good, too, with a chunk of cheddar—and I sipped coffee along with it. Over the rim of the cup, I cocked my head at her and shook it, slowly, from one side to the other.

"I can get you off duty for a day," she told me. "There will be no harm done."

"Sorry. I'm interested in the results of the tests. Let's make it this weekend."

She seemed to think about this for a while.

"All right," she said finally, and I nodded and continued with my dessert.

The "all right" instead of a "yes" or an "okay" or a "sure" must have been a key word of some sort. Or perhaps it was something else that she did or said. I don't know. I don't care any more.

When we left the commissary, she was slightly ahead of me—as I had opened the door for her—and a man moved in from either side.

She stopped and turned.

"Don't bother saying it," I said. "I wasn't quick enough, so I'm under arrest. Please don't recite my rights. I know what they are," and I raised my hands when I saw the steel in one man's hand. "Merry Christmas," I added.

But she recited my rights anyway, and I stared at her all the while. She didn't meet my eyes.

Hell, the whole proposition had been too good to be true. I didn't think she was very used to the role she had played, though—and I wondered, idly, whether she would have gone through with it, if circumstances dictated. She had been right about my job aboard the *Aquina* being ended, however. I would have to be moving along, and seeing that Albert Schweitzer died within the next twenty-four hours.

"You *are* going to Spitzbergen tonight," she said, "where there are better facilities for questioning you."

How was I going to manage it? Well—

As if reading my thoughts, she said, "Since you seem to be somewhat dangerous, I wish to advise you that your escorts are highly trained men."

"Then you won't be coming with me, after all?"

"I'm afraid not."

"Too bad. Then this is going to have to be 'Goodbye.' I'd like to have gotten to know you somewhat better."

"That meant nothing!" she said. "It was just to get you there."

"Maybe. But you will always wonder, and now you will never know."

"I am afraid we are going to have to handcuff you," said one of the men.

"Of course."

I held my hands out and he said, almost apologetically, "No, sir. Behind your back, please."

So I did, but I watched the men move in and I got a look at the cuffs. They were kind of old-fashioned. Government budgets generally produce such handy savings. If I bent over backward, I could step over them, and then they would be in front of me. Give me, say, twenty seconds . . .

"One thing," I asked. "Just for the sake of curiosity and because I told it to you straight. Did you ever find out why those two guys broke into my room to question me, and what they really wanted? If you're allowed to tell me, I would like to know, because it made for some rough sleeping."

She bit her lip, thought a moment, I guess, then said, "They were from New Salem—a bubble city off the North American continental shelf. They were afraid that RUMOKO would crack their dome."

"Did it?" I asked.

She paused.

"We don't know yet," she said. "The place has been silent for a while. We have tried to get through to them, but there seems to be some interference."

"What do you mean by that?"

"We have not yet succeeded in reestablishing contact."

"You mean to say that we might have killed a city?"

"No. The chances were minimal, according to the scientists."

"*Your* scientists," I said. "Theirs must have felt differently about it."

"Of course," she told me. "There are always obstructionists. They sent saboteurs because they did not trust our scientists. The inference—"

"I'm sorry," I said.

"For what?"

"That I put a guy into a shower. —Okay. Thanks. I can read all about it in the papers. Send me to Spitzbergen now."

"Please," she said. "I do what I must. I think it's right. You may be as clean as snow and swansdown. If that is the case, they will know in a very short time, Al. Then —then I'd like you to bear in mind that what I said before may still be good."

I chuckled.

"Sure, and I've already said, 'Good-bye.' Thanks for answering my question, though."

"Don't hate me."

"I don't. But I could never trust you."

She turned away.

"Good night, " I said.

And they escorted me to the helicopter. They helped me aboard. There were just the two of them and the pilot.

"She liked you," said the man with the gun.

"No." I said.

"If she's right and you're clean, will you see her again?"

"I'll never see her again," I said.

He seated me, to the rear of the craft. Then he and his buddy took window seats and gave a signal.

The engines throbbed, and suddenly we rose.

In the distance, RUMOKO rumbled, burned, and spat.

Eva, I am sorry. I didn't know. I'd never guessed it might have done what it did.

"You're supposed to be dangerous," said the man on my right. "Please don't try anything."

Ave, atque, avatque, I said, in my heart of hearts, like.

Twenty-four hours, I told Schweitzer.

After I collected my money from Walsh, I returned to the *Proteus* and practiced meditation for a few days. Since it did not produce the desired results, I went up and got drunk with Bill Mellings. After all, I had used his equipment to kill Schweitzer. I didn't tell him anything, except for a made-up story about a *ni-hi* girl with large mammaries.

Then we went fishing, two weeks' worth.

I did not exist any longer. I had erased Albert Schweitzer from the world. I kept telling myself that I did not want to exist any longer.

If you have to murder a man—*have to,* I mean, like no choice in the matter—I feel that it should be a bloody and horrible thing, so that it burns itself into your soul and gives you a better appreciation of the value of human existence.

It had not been that way, however.

It had been quiet and viral. It was a thing to which I have immunized myself, but of which very few other persons have even heard. I had opened my ring and released the spores. That was all. I had never known the names of my escorts or the pilot. I had not even had a good look at their faces.

It had killed them within thirty seconds, and I had the

cuffs off in less than the twenty seconds I'd guessed.

I crashed the 'copter on the beach, sprained my right wrist doing it, got the hell out of the vehicle, and started walking.

They'd look like myocardial infarcts or arteriosclerotic brain syndromes—depending on how it hit them.

Which meant I should lay low for a while. I value my own existence slightly more than that of anyone who wishes to disturb it. This does not mean that I didn't feel like hell, though.

Carol will suspect, I think, but Central only buys facts. And I saw that there was enough sea water in the plane to take care of the spores. No test known to man could prove that I had murdered them.

The body of Albert Schweitzer had doubtless been washed out to sea through the sprung door.

If I ever meet with anybody who had known Al, so briefly, I'd be somebody else by then—with appropriate identification—and that person would be mistaken.

Very neat. But maybe I'm in the wrong line of work. I *still* feel like hell.

RUMOKO From All Those Fathoms fumed and grew like those Hollywood monsters that used to get blamed on science fiction. In a few months, it was predicted, its fires would desist. A layer of soil would then be imported, spread, and migrating birds would be encouraged to stop and rest, maybe nest, and to use the place as a lavatory. Mutant red mangroves would be rooted there, linking the sea and the land. Insects would even be brought aboard. One day, according to theory, it would be a habitable island. One other day, it would be one of a chain of habitable islands.

A double-pronged answer to the population problem, you might say: create a new place for men to live, and in doing so kill off a crowd of them living elsewhere.

Yes, the seismic shocks had cracked New Salem's dome. Many people had died.

And Project RUMOKO's *second* son is nevertheless scheduled for next summer.

The people in Baltimore II are worried, but the Congressional investigation showed that the fault lay with the constructors of New Salem, who should have provided against the vicissitudes. The courts held several of the contractors liable, and two of them went into receivership despite the connections that had gotten them the contracts in the first place.

It ain't pretty, and it's big, and I sort of wish I had never put that guy into the shower. He is all alive and well, I understand—a New Salem man—but I know that he will never be the same.

More precautions are supposed to be taken with the next one—whatever that means. I do not trust these precautions worth a damn. But then, I do not trust anything anymore.

If another bubble city goes, as yours did, Eva, I think it will slow things down. But I do not believe it will stop the RUMOKO Project. I think they will find another excuse then. I think they will try for a third one after that.

While it has been proved that we can create such things, I do not believe that the answer to our population problem lies in the manufacturing of new lands. No.

Offhand, I would say that since everything else is controlled these days, we might as well do it with the population, too. I will even get myself an identity— many identities, in fact—and vote for it, if it ever comes to a referendum. And I submit that there should be more bubble cities, and increased appropriations with respect to the exploration of outer space. But no more RUMOKO's. No.

Despite past reservations, I am taking on a free one. Walsh will never know. Hopefully, no one will. I am no altruist, but I guess I owe something to the race that I leech off of. After all, I was once a member. . . .

Taking advantage of my nonexistence, I am going to sabotage that bastard so well that it will be the last.

How?

I will see that it is a Krakatoa, at least. As a result of the last one, Central knows a lot more about magma— and as a result of this, so do I.

I will manipulate the charge, probably even make it a multiple.

When that baby goes off, I will have arranged for it to be the worst seismic disturbance in the memory of man. It should not be too difficult to do.

I could possibly murder thousands of people by this action—and certainly I will kill some. However, RU-MOKO in its shattering of New Salem scared the hell out of so many folks that I think RUMOKO II will scare even more. I am hoping that there will be a lot of topside vacations about that time. Add to this the fact that I know how rumors get started, and I can do it myself. I will.

I am at least going to clear the decks as much as I can.

They will get results, all right—the planners—like a Mount Everest in the middle of the Atlantic and some fractured domes. Laugh that off, and you are a good man.

I baited the line and threw it overboard. Bill took a drink of orange juice and I took a drag on my cigarette.

"You're a consulting engineer these days?" he asked.

"Yeah."

"What are you up to now?"

"I've got a job in mind. Kind of tricky."

"Will you take it?"

"Yes."

"I sometimes wish I had something going for me now —the way you do."

"Don't. It's not worth it."

I looked out over the dark waters, able to bear prodigies. The morning sun was just licking the waves, and my decision was, like, solid. The wind was chilly and pleasant. The sky was going to be beautiful. I could tell from the breaks in the cloud cover.

"It sounds interesting. This is demolition work, you say?"

And I, Judas Iscariot, turned a glance his way and said, "Pass me the bait can, please. I think I've got something on the line."

"Me, too. Wait a minute."

The day, like a mess of silver dollars, fell upon the deck.

I landed mine and hit it on the back of the head with the stick, to be merciful.

I kept telling myself that I did not exist. I hope it is true, even though I feel that it is not. I seem to see old Colgate's face beneath an occasional whitecap.

Eva, Eva . . .

Forgive me, my Eva. I would welcome your hand on my brow.

It is pretty, the silver. The waves are blue and green this morning, and God! how lovely the light!

"Here's the bait."

"Thanks."

I took it and we drifted.

Eventually, everybody dies, I noted. But it did not make me feel any better.

But nothing, really, could.

The next card will be for Christmas, as usual, Don, one year late this time around.

Never ask me why.

PART TWO

'Kjwalll'kje'k'koothaïlll'kje'k

After everyone had departed, the statements been taken, the remains of the remains removed—long after that, as the night hung late, clear, clean, with its bright multitudes doubled in their pulsing within the cool flow of the Gulf Stream about the station, I sat in a deck chair on the small patio behind my quarters, drinking a can of beer and watching the stars go by.

My feelings were an uncomfortable mixture, and I had not quite decided what to do with what was left.

It was awkward. I could make things neat and tidy again by deciding to forget the small inexplicables. I had accomplished what I had set out to do. I needed but stamp CLOSED on my mental file, go away, collect my fee and live happily, relatively speaking, ever after.

No one would ever know or, for that matter, care about the little things that still bothered me. I was under no obligation to pursue matters beyond this point.

Except . . .

Maybe it *is* an obligation. At least, at times it became a compulsion, and one might as well salve one's notions of duty and free will by using the pleasanter term.

It? The possession of a primate forebrain, I mean, with a deep curiosity wrinkle furrowing it for better or worse.

I had to remain about the station a while longer anyway, for appearances' sake.

I took another sip of beer.

65

Yes, I wanted more answers. To dump into the bottomless wrinkle up front there.

I might as well look around a bit more. Yes, I decided, I would.

I withdrew a cigarette and moved to light it. Then the flame caught my attention.

I stared at the flowing tongue of light, illuminating the palm and curved fingers of my left hand, raised to shield it from the night breeze. It seemed as pure as the starfires themselves, a molten, buttery thing, touched with orange, haloed blue, the intermittently exposed cherry-colored wick glowing, half-hidden, like a soul. And then the music began. . . .

Music was the best term I had for it, because of some similarity of essence, although it was actually like nothing I had ever experienced before. For one thing, it was not truly sonic. It came into me as a memory comes, without benefit of external stimulus—but lacking the Lucite layer of self-consciousness that turns thought to recollection by touching it with time—as in a dream. Then, something suspended, something released, my feelings began to move to the effect. Not emotions, nothing that specific, but rather a growing sense of euphoria, delight, wonder, all poured together into a common body with the tide rising. What the progressions, what the combinations—what the thing was, truly—I did not know. It was an intense beauty, a beautiful intensity, however, and I was part of it. It was as if I were experiencing something no man had ever known before, something cosmic, magnificent, ubiquitous yet commonly ignored.

And it was with a peculiarly ambiguous effort, following a barely perceptible decision, that I twitched the fingers of my left hand sufficiently to bring them into the flame itself.

The pain broke the dream momentarily, and I snapped the lighter closed as I sprang to my feet, a gaggle of guesses passing through my head. I turned and ran across that humming artificial islet, heading for the small, dark cluster of buildings that held the museum, library, offices.

But even as I moved, something came to me again. Only this time it was not the glorious, musiclike sensation that had touched me moments earlier. Now it was sinister, bringing a fear that was none the less real for my knowing it to be irrational, to the accompaniment of sensory distortions that must have caused me to reel as I ran. The surface on which I moved buckled and swayed; the stars, the buildings, the ocean—everything —advanced and retreated in random, nauseating patterns of attack. I fell several times, recovered, rushed onward. Some of the distance I know that I crawled. Closing my eyes did no good, for everything was warped, throbbing, shifting, and awful inside as well as out.

It was only a few hundred yards, though, no matter what the signs and portents might say, and finally I rested my hands against the wall, worked my way to the door, opened it, and passed within.

Another door and I was into the library. For years, it seemed, I fumbled to switch on the light.

I staggered to the desk, fought with a drawer, wrestled a screwdriver out of it.

Then on my hands and knees, gritting my teeth, I crossed to the remote-access terminal of the Information Network. Slapping at the console's control board, I succeeded in tripping the switches that brought it to life.

Then, still on my knees, holding the screwdriver with both hands, I got the left side panel off the thing. It fell to the floor with a sound that drove spikes into my head. But the components were exposed. Three little changes and I could transmit, something that would eventually wind up in Central. I resolved that I would make those changes and send the two most damaging pieces of information I could guess at to the place where they might eventually be retrived in association with something sufficiently similar to one day cause a query, a query that would hopefully lead to the destruction of that for which I was currently being tormented.

"I mean it!" I said aloud. "Stop right now! Or I'll do it!"

. . . And it was like taking off a pair of unfamiliar glasses: rampant reality.

I climbed to my feet, shut down the board.

The next thing, I decided, was to have that cigarette I had wanted in the first place.

With my third puff, I heard the outer door open and close.

Dr. Barthelme, short, tan, gray on top and wiry, entered the room, blue eyes wide, one hand partly raised.

"Jim! What's wrong?" he said.

"Nothing," I replied. "Nothing."

"I saw you running. I saw you fall."

"Yes. I decided to sprint over here. I slipped. Pulled a muscle. It's all right."

"Why the rush?"

"Nerves. I'm still edgy, upset. I had to run or something, to get it out of my system. Decided to run over and get a book. Something to read myself to sleep with."

"I can get you a tranquilizer."

"No, that's all right. Thanks. I'd rather not."

"What were you doing to the machine? We're not supposed to fool with—"

"The side panel fell off when I went past it. I was just going to put it back on." I waved the screwdriver. "The little set-screws must have jiggled loose."

"Oh."

I stooped and fitted it back into place. As I was tightening the screws, the telephone rang. Barthelme crossed to the desk, poked an extension button, and answered it.

After a moment, he said, "Yes, just a minute," and turned. "It's for you."

"Really?"

I rose, moved to the desk, took the receiver, dropping the screwdriver back into the drawer and closing it.

"Hello?" I said.

"All right," said the voice. "I think we had better talk. Will you come and see me now?"

"Where are you?"

"At home."

"All right. I'll come."

I hung up.

"Don't need that book after all," I said. "I'm going over to Andros for a while."

"It's pretty late. Are you certain you feel up to it?"

"Oh, I feel fine now," I said. "Sorry to have worried you."

He seemed to relax. At least, he sagged and smiled faintly.

"Maybe *I* should go take the trank," he said. "Everything that's happened . . . You know. You scared me."

"Well, what's happened has happened. It's all over, done."

"You're right, of course. . . . Well, have a good time, whatever."

He turned toward the door and I followed him out, extinguishing the light as I passed it.

"Good night, then."

"Good night."

He headed back toward his quarters, and I made my way down to the docking area, decided on the *Isabella*, got in. Moments later, I was crossing over, still wondering. Curiosity may ultimately prove nature's way of dealing with the population problem.

It was on May Day—not all that long ago, though it seems so—that I sat to the rear of the bar at Captain Tony's in Key West, to the right, near to the fireplace, drinking one of my seasonal beers. It was a little after eleven, and I had about decided that this one was a write-off, when Don came in through the big open front of the place. He glanced around, his eyes passing over me, located a vacant stool near the forward corner of the bar, took it, and ordered something. There were too many people between us, and the group had returned to the stage at the rear of the room behind me and begun another set, with a loud opening number. So, for a time, we just sat there—wondering, I guess.

After ten or fifteen minutes, he got to his feet and made his way back to the rest room, passing around the far side of the bar. A short while later, he returned, moving around my side. I felt his hand on my shoulder.

"Bill!" he said. "What are you doing down here?"

I turned, regarded him, grinned.

"Sam! Good Lord!"

We shook hands. Then, "Too noisy in here to talk," he said. "Let's go someplace else."

"Good idea."

After a time, we found ourselves on a dim and deserted stretch of beach, smelling the salty breath of the ocean, listening to it, and feeling an occasional droplet. We halted, and I lit a cigarette.

"Did you know that the Florida current carries over two million tons of uranium past here every year?" he said.

"To be honest, no," I told him

"Well, it does. —What do you know about dolphins?"

"That's better," I said. "They are beautiful, friendly creatures, so well adapted to their environment that they don't have to mess it up in order to lead the life they seem to enjoy. They are highly intelligent, they're cooperative, and they seem totally lacking in all areas of maliciousness. They—"

"That's enough," and he raised his hand. "You like dolphins. I knew you would say that. You sometimes remind me of one—swimming through life, not leaving traces, retrieving things for me."

"Keep me in fish. That's all."

He nodded.

"The usual arrangement. But this one should be a relatively easy, yes-or-no thing, and not take you too long. It's quite near here, as a matter of fact, and the incident is only a few days old."

"Oh! What's involved?"

"I'd like to clear a gang of dolphins of a homicide charge," he said.

If he expected me to say something, he he was disappointed. I was thinking, recalling a news account from the previous week. Two scuba-clad swimmers had been killed in one of the undersea parks to the east, at about the same time that some very peculiar activity on the part of dolphins was being observed in the same area. The men had been bitten and chewed by something possessing a jaw configuration approximating that of *Tursiops truncatus*, the bottle-nosed dolphin, a normal visitor and sometime resident of these same parks. The particular park in which the incident occurred had been closed until further notice. There were no witnesses to the attack, as I recalled, and I had not come across any follow-up story.

"I'm serious," he finally said.

"One of those guys was a qualified guide who knew the area, wasn't he?"

He brightened, there in the dark.

"Yes," he said. "Michael Thornley. He used to do some moonlighting as a guide. He was a full-time employee of the Beltrane Processing people. Did underwater repair and maintenance at their extraction plants. Ex-Navy. Frogman. Extremely qualified. The other fellow was a landlubber friend of his from Andros. Rudy Myers. They went out together at an odd hour, stayed rather long. In the meantime, several dolphins were seen getting the hell out, fast. They leaped the 'wall,' instead of passing through the locks. Others used the normal exits. These were blinking on and off like mad. In a matter of a few minutes, actually, every dolphin in the park had apparently departed. When an employee went looking for Mike and Rudy, he found them dead."

"Where do you come into the picture?"

"The Institute of Delphinological Studies does not appreciate the bad press this gives their subject. They maintain there has never been an authenticated case of an unprovoked attack by a dolphin on a human being. They are anxious not to have this go on record as one, if it really isn't."

"Well, it hasn't actually been established. Perhaps something else did it. Scared the dolphins, too."

"I have no idea," he said, lighting a cigarette of his own. "But it was not all that long ago that the killing of dolphins was finally made illegal throughout the world, and that the pioneer work of people like Lilly came to be appreciated, with a really large-scale project set up for the assessment of the creature. They have come up with some amazing results, as you must know. It is no longer a question of trying to demonstrate whether a dolphin is as intelligent as a man. It has been established that they are highly intelligent—although their minds work along radically different lines, so that there probably never can be a true comparison. This is the basic reason for the continuing communication problems, and it is also a matter of which the general public is pretty much aware. Given this, our client does not like the inferences that could be drawn from the incident—namely, that powerful, free-ranging creatures of this order of intelligence could become hostile to man."

"So the Institute hired you to look into it?"

"Not officially. I was approached because the character of the thing smacks of my sort of investigation specialties as well as the scientific. Mainly, though, it was because of the urgings of a wealthy little old lady who may someday leave the Institute a fortune: Mrs. Lydia Barnes, former president of the Friends of the Dolphin Society—the citizen group that had lobbied for the initial dolphin legislation years ago. She is really paying my fee."

"What sort of place in the picture did you have in mind for me?"

"Beltrane will want a replacement for Michael Thornley. Do you think you could get the job?"

"Maybe. Tell me more about Beltrane and the parks."

"Well," he said, "I guess it was a generation or so back that Dr. Spencer at Harwell demonstrated that titanium hydroxide would create a chemical reaction that separated uranyl ions from seawater. It was costly, though, and it was not until years later that Samuel Beltrane came along with his screening technique, founded a small company, and quickly turned it into a large one, with uranium-extraction stations all along this piece of the Gulf Stream. While his process was quite clean, environmentally speaking, he was setting up in business at a time when public pressure on industry was such that some gesture of ecological concern was pretty much *de rigueur*. So he threw a lot of money, equipment, and man-hours into the setting up of the four undersea parks in the vicinity of the island of Andros. A section of the barrier reef makes one of them especially attractive. He got a nice tax break on the deal. Deserved, though, I'd say. He cooperated with the dolphin studies people, and labs were set up for them in the parks. Each of the four areas is enclosed by a sonic 'wall,' a sound barrier that keeps everything outside out and everything inside in, in terms of the larger creatures. Except for men and dolphins. At a number of points, the 'wall' possesses 'sound locks'—a pair of sonic curtains, several meters apart—which are operated by means of a simple control located on the bottom. Dolphins are capable of teaching one another how to use it, and they are quite good about closing the door behind them. They come and go, visiting the labs at will, both learning from and, I guess, teaching the investigators."

"Stop," I said. "What about sharks?"

"They were removed from the parks first thing. The dolphins even helped chase them out. It has been over a decade now since the last one was put out."

"I see. What say does the company have in running the parks?"

"None, really. They service the equipment now, that's all."

"Do many of the Beltrane people work as park guides too?"

"A few, part-time. They are in the area, they know it well, they have all the necessary skills."

"I would like to see whatever medical reports there were."

"I have them here, complete with photos of the bodies."

"What about the man from Andros—Rudy Myers? What did he do?"

"He'd trained as a nurse. Worked in several homes for the aged. Taken in a couple of times on charges of stealing from the patients. Charges dropped once. A suspended sentence the second time. Sort of blackballed from that line of work afterward. That was six or seven years back. Held a variety of small jobs then and kept a clean record. He had been working on the island for the past couple of years in a sort of bar."

"What do you mean 'sort of bar'?"

"It has only an alcohol license, but it serves drugs, too. It's way out in the boonies, though, so nobody's ever raised a fuss."

"What's the place called?"

"The Chickcharny."

"What's that mean?"

"A piece of local folklore. A chickcharny is a sort of tree spirit. Mischievous. Like an elf."

"Colorful enough, I guess. —Isn't Andros where Martha Millay, the photographer, makes her home?"

"Yes, it is."

"I'm a fan of hers. I like underwater photography, and hers is always good. In fact, she did several books on dolphins. Has anyone thought to ask her opinion of the killings?"

"She's been away."

"Oh. Hope she gets back soon. I'd like to meet her."

"Then you will take the job?"

"Yes, I need one just now."

He reached into his jacket, withdrew a heavy envelope, passed it to me.

"There you have copies of everything I have. Needless to say—"

"Needless to say," I said, "the life of a mayfly will be as eternity to them."

I slipped it into my own jacket and turned away.

"Be seeing you," I said.

"Leaving already?"

"I've a lot to do."

"Good luck, then."

"Thanks."

I went left and he went right, and that was that for then.

Station One was something of a nerve center for the area. That is, it was larger than the other extraction plants and contained the field office, several laboratories, a library, a museum, a dispensary, living quarters, and a few recreational features. It was an artificial island, a fixed platform about seven hundred feet across, and it monitored and serviced eight other plants within the area. It was within sight of Andros, largest of the Bahama Islands, and if you like plenty of water about you, which I do, you would find the prospect peaceful and more than a little attractive.

After the tour and introductions that first day, I learned that my duties were about one-third routine and two-thirds response to circumstances. The routine part was inspection and preventive maintenance. The rest was unforeseen repair, retrieval, and replacement work —general underwater handyman stuff whenever the necessity arose.

It was Dr. Leonard Barthelme, the Area Director, who met me and showed me around. A pleasant little fellow who seemed to enjoy talking about his work, middle-aged, a widower, he had made his home at Station One for almost five years. The first person to whom he introduced me was Frank Cashel, whom we found in the main laboratory, eating a sandwich and waiting for some test to run its course.

Frank swallowed and smiled, rose, and shook hands with me as Barthelme explained, "This is the new man, James Madison."

He was dark, with a touch of gray here and there, a few creases accentuating a ruggedness of jawline and cheekbone, the beginnings of a bulge above his belt.

"Glad to have you around," he said. "Keep an eye out for pretty rocks, and bring me a branch of coral every now and then. We'll get along fine."

"Frank's hobby is collecting minerals," Barthelme said. "The display in the museum is his. We'll pass that way in a few minutes and you can see it. Quite interesting."

I nodded.

"Okay. I'll remember. See what I can find you."

"Know anything about the subject?" Frank asked me.

"A little. I used to be something of a rock hound."

"Well, I'd appreciate it."

As we walked away, Barthelme remarked, "He makes some money on the side selling specimens at gem shows. I would bear that in mind before I gave him too much in the way of my spare time, or samples."

"Oh."

"What I mean is, if you feel like going in for that sort of thing on a more than occasional basis, you ought to make it clear that you want a percentage."

"I see. Thanks."

"Don't misunderstand me," he said. "He's a fine fellow. Just a little absentminded."

"How long has he been out here?"

"Around two years. Geophysicist. Very solid."

We stopped by the equipment shed then, where I met Andy Deems and Paul Carter: the former, thin and somewhat sinister in appearance because of a scribbling of scars on his left cheek, which a full beard did not completely conceal; the latter, tall, fair, smooth-faced, and somewhere between husky and fat. They were cleaning some tanks when we entered, and wiped their hands, shook mine, and said they were glad to meet me. They both did the same sort of work I would be doing, the normal staffing calling for four of us, working in pairs. The fourth man was Paul Vallons, who was currently out with Ronald Davies, the boatmaster, replacing an instrument package in a sampler buoy. Paul, I learned, had been Mike's partner, the two of them having been friends since their Navy days. I would be working with him much of the time.

"You will soon be reduced to this miserable state yourself," Carter said cheerfully, as we were leaving. "Enjoy your morning. Gather rosebuds."

"You are miserable because you sweat most obscenely," Deems observed.

"Tell it to my glands."

As we crossed the islet, Barthelme observed that Deems was the most capable underwater man he had ever met. He had lived in one of the bubble cities for a time, lost his wife and daughter in the RUMOKO II disaster, and come topside to stay. Carter had come across from the West Coast about five months ago, immediately following a divorce or separation he did not care to talk about. He had been employed by Beltrane out there and had requested a transfer.

Barthelme took me through the second lab, which was vacant just then, so that I could admire the large, illuminated map of the seas about Andros, beads of light indicating the disposition and well-being of the devices that maintained the sonic 'walls' about the parks and stations. I saw that we were enclosed by a boundary that took in the nearest park also.

"In which one was the accident?" I asked.

He turned and studied my face, then pointed, indicating our own.

"It was farther in, over there," he said. "Toward the northeast end of the park. What have you heard about it?"

"Just the news report," I said. "Has anything new been discovered?"

"No. Nothing."

With my fingertip, I traced the reversed L of lights that outlined the area.

"No holes in the 'wall'?" I asked.

"There haven't been any equipment failures for a long while."

"Do you think it was a dolphin?"

He shrugged. Then, "I'm a chemist," he said, "not a dolphin specialist. But it strikes me, from everything I've read, that there are dolphins and there are dolphins. The average dolphin seems to be quite pacific, with an intelligence possibly equivalent to our own. Also, they should follow the same old normal distribution curve—the bulk of them in the middle, a few morons on one end, a few geniuses on the other. Perhaps a feebleminded dolphin who was not responsible for his actions did it. Or a Raskolnikov dolphin. Most of what is known about them comes from a study of average specimens. Statistically, in the relatively brief while such investigations have been going on, this has to be so. What do we know of their psychiatric abnormalities? Nothing, really." He shrugged again. "So yes, I think it is possible," he finished.

I was thinking then of a bubble city and some people I had never met, and I wondered whether dolphins ever felt rotten, guilty, and miserable as hell over anything they had done. I sent that thought back where it had come from, just as he said, "I hope you are not worried . . . ?"

"Curious," I said. "But concerned, too. Naturally."

He turned and, as I followed him to the door, said, "Well, you have to remember first that it was a good distance to the northeast, in the park proper. We have nothing operating over there, so your duties should not take you anywhere near the place where it occurred. Second, a team from the Institute of Delphinological Studies is searching the entire area, including our annex here, with underwater detection equipment. Third, until further notice there will be a continuing sonar scan about any area where one of our people has to submerge himself—and a shark cage and submersible decompression chamber will go along on all deep dives, just in case. The locks have all been closed until this is settled. And you will be given a weapon—a long metal tube carrying a charge and a shell—that should be capable of dispatching an angry dolphin or a shark."

I nodded.

"Okay," I said, as we headed toward the next cluster of buildings. "That makes me feel a lot better."

"I was going to get around to that in a little while anyway," he said. "I was looking for the best way to get into it, though. I feel better, too—this part is offices. Should be empty now."

He pulled open the door and I followed him through: desks, partitions, filing cabinets, office machines, water cooler—nothing unusual—and, as he had said, quite deserted. We passed along its center aisle and out the door at its far end, where we crossed the narrow breezeway that separated it from the adjacent building. We entered there.

"This is our museum," he said. "Sam Beltrane thought it would be nice to have a small one to show visitors. Full of sea things as well as a few models of our equipment."

Nodding, I looked about. At least the model equipment did not dominate, as I would have expected. The floor was covered with green indoor-outdoor carpeting, and a miniature version of the station itself occupied a tablelike frame near the front door, all of its underside equipment exposed. Shelves on the wall behind it held larger-scale versions of some of the more important components, placarded with a paragraph or two of explanation and history. There were an antique cannon, two lantern frames, several belt buckles, a few coins, and some corroded utensils displayed nearby, salvaged from a centuries-old vessel that still lay on the bottom not very far from the station, according to the plaque. On the opposite wall, with several of the larger ones set up on frames before it, was a display of marine skeletons accompanied by colored sketches of the fully fleshed and finned versions, ranging from tiny spinefish to a dolphin, along with a full-sized mock-up of a shark, which I determined to come back and compare a little more carefully on my own time. There was a large section containing Frank Cashel's mineral display, neatly mounted and labeled, separated from the fish by a window and overlooked by a slightly awkward but still attractive watercolor titled *Miami Skyline*, with the name "Cashel" scrawled in its lower corner.

"Oh, Frank paints," I said. "Not bad."

"No, that's his wife, Linda's," he replied. "You will meet her in just a minute. She should be next door. She runs the library and takes care of all our clerical work."

So we passed through the door that led to the library and I saw Linda Cashel. She was seated at a desk, writing, and she looked up as we entered. She appeared to be in her mid-twenties. Her hair was long, sun-bleached, pulled back, held with a jeweled clip. Blue eyes, in a longish face with a cleft chin, a slightly upturned nose, a sprinkling of freckles, and some very even, very white teeth were displayed as Barthelme greeted her and introduced us.

". . . Anytime you want a book," she said.

I looked around at the shelves, the cases, the machines.

"We keep good copies of the standard reference works we use a lot," she said. "I can get facsimile copies of anything else on a day's notice. There are some shelves of general fiction and light stuff over there." She indicated a rack beside the front window. "Then there are those banks of cassettes to your right, mostly undersea noises—fish sounds and such, for part of a continuing study we do for the National Science Foundation—and the last bank is music, for our own enjoyment. Everything is catalogued here." She rose and slapped a file unit, indicated an index key taped to its side. "If you want to take something out and nobody's around, I would appreciate it if you would record its number, your name, and the date in this book." She glanced at a ledger on the corner of her desk. "And if you want to keep anything longer than a week, please mention it to me. There is also a tool chest in the bottom drawer, in case you ever need a pair of pliers. Remember to put them back. That covers everything I can think of," she said. "Any questions?"

"Doing much painting these days?" I asked.

"Oh," she said, reseating herself, "you saw my skyline. I'm afraid next door is the only museum I'll ever get into. I've pretty much quit. I know I'm not that good."

"I rather liked it."

She twisted her mouth.

"When I'm older and wiser and somewhere else, maybe I'll try again. I've done everything I care to with water and shorelines."

I smiled because I couldn't think of anything else to say, and she did the same. Then we left, and Barthelme gave me the rest of the morning off to get settled in my cottage, which had been Michael Thornley's quarters. I went and did that.

After lunch, I went to work with Deems and Carter in the equipment shed. As a result, we finished early. Since it was still too soon to think of dinner, they offered to take me for a swim, to see the sunken ship.

It was about a quarter mile to the south, outside the "wall," perhaps twenty fathoms down—what was left of it—and eerie, as such things always are, in the wavering beams we extended. A broken mast, a snapped bowsprit, a section of deck planking and smashed gunwale visible above the mud, an agitated horde of little fish we had disturbed at whatever they were about within and near the hulk, a partial curtain of weeds drawn and redrawn by the currents, and that was all that remained of someone's hopes for a successful voyage, some shipbuilders' labors, and possibly a number of people whose last impressions were of storm or sword, and then the gray, blue, green, sudden springs uncoiling, cold.

Or maybe they made it over to Andros and dinner, as we did later. We ate in a red-and-white-checked-tablecloth sort of place near to the shore, where just about everything man-made clung, the interior of Andros being packed with mangrove swamps, mahogany and pine forests, doves, ducks, quail, pigeons, and chickcharnies. The food was good; I was hungry.

We sat for a time afterward, smoking and talking. I still had not met Paul Vallons, but I was scheduled to work with him the following day. I asked Deems what he was like.

"Big fellow," he said, "around your size, only he's good-looking. Kind of reserved. Fine diver. He and Mike used to take off every weekend, go helling around the Caribbean. Had a girl on every island, I'll bet."

"How's he—taking things?"

"Pretty well, I guess. Like I said, he's kind of reserved, doesn't show his feelings much. He and Mike had been friends for years."

"What do you think got Mike?"

Carter broke in then.

"One of those damned dolphins," he said. "We should never have started fooling with them. One of them came up under me once, damn near ruptured me."

"They're playful," Deems said. "It didn't mean any harm."

"I think it did. —And that slick skin of theirs reminds me of a wet balloon. Sickening!"

"You're prejudiced. They're friendly as puppies. It probably goes back to some sexual hangup."

"Crap!" Carter said. "They—"

Since I had gotten it started, I felt obligated to change the subject. So I asked whether it was true that Martha Millay lived nearby.

"Yes," Deems said, taking hold of the opportunity. "She has a place about four miles down the coast from here. Very neat, I understand, though I've only seen it from the water. Her own little port. She has a hydrofoil, a sailboat, a good-sized cabin cruiser, and a couple little power launches. Lives alone in a long, low building right smack on the water. Not even a road out that way."

"I've admired her work for a long while. I'd like to meet her sometime."

He shook his head.

"I'll bet you never do. She doesn't like people. Doesn't have a listed phone."

"That's a pity. Any idea why she's that way?"

"Well . . ."

"She's deformed," Carter said. "I met her once, on the water. She was at anchor and I was going past on my way to one of the stations. That was before I knew about her, so I went near, just to say hello. She was taking pictures through the glass bottom of her boat, and when she saw me she started to scream and holler for me to get away, that I was scaring the fish. And she snatched up a tarp and pulled it over her legs. I got a look, though. She's a nice, normal-looking woman from the waist up, but her hips and legs are all twisted and ugly. I was sorry I'd embarrassed her. I was just as embarrassed myself, and I didn't know what to say. So I yelled, 'Sorry,' and waved and kept going."

"I heard she can't walk at all," Deems said, "though she is supposed to be an excellent swimmer. I've never seen her myself."

"Was she in some sort of accident, do you know?"

"Not as I understand it," he said. "She is half Japanese, and the story I heard is that her mother was a Hiroshima baby. Some sort of genetic damage."

"Pity."

"Yes."

We settled up and headed back. Later, I lay awake for a long while, thinking of dolphins, sunken ships, drowned people, half people, and the Gulf Stream, which kept talking to me through the window. Finally, I listened to it, and it took hold of me and we drifted away together into the darkness to wherever it finally goes.

Paul Vallons was, as Andy Deems had said, around my size and good-looking, in a dark, clothing-advertisement sort of way. Another twenty years and he would probably even look distinguished. Some guys win all the way around. Deems had also been right about his reserve. He was not especially talkative, although he managed this without seeming unfriendly. As for his diving prowess, I was unable to confirm it that first day I worked with him, for we pulled shore duty while Deems and Carter got sent over to Station Three. Back to the equipment shed . . .

I did not think it a good idea to ask him about his late buddy, or dolphins, which pretty much confined me conversation-wise to the business at hand and a few generalities. Thus was the morning passed.

After lunch, though, as I began thinking ahead, going over my plans for that evening, I decided he would be as good as anyone when it came to getting directions to the Chickcharny.

He lowered the valve he had been cleaning and stared at me.

"What do you want to go to that dive for?" he asked.

"Heard the place mentioned," I said. "Like to see it."

"They serve drugs without a license," he told me. "No inspection. If you like the stuff, you have no guarantee you won't be served some crap the village idiot cooks up in an outhouse."

"Then I'll stick to beer. Still like to see the place."

He shrugged.

"Not that much to look at. But here——"

He wiped his hands, tore an old leaf from the back of the wall calendar, and sketched me a quick map. I saw that it was a bit inland, toward the birds and mangroves, muck and mahogany. It was also somewhat to the south of the place I had been the previous evening. It was located on a stream, built up on pilings out over the water, he said, and I could take a boat right up to the pier that adjoined it.

"Think I'll go over tonight," I said.

"Remember what I said."

I nodded as I tucked away the map.

The afternoon passed quickly. There came a massing of clouds, a brief rainfall—about a quarter hour's worth —and then the sun returned to dry the decks and warm the just-rinsed world. Again, the workday ended early for me, by virtue of our having run out of business. I showered quickly, put on fresh clothes, and went to see about getting the use of a light boat.

Ronald Davies, a tall, thin-haired man with a New England accent, said I could take the speedboat called *Isabella*, complained about his arthritis, and told me to have a good time. I nodded, turned her toward Andros, and sputtered away, hoping the Chickcharny included food among its inducements, as I did not want to waste time by stopping elsewhere.

The sea was calm and the gulls dipped and pivoted, uttering hoarse cries, as I spread the wings of my wake across their preserve. I really had no idea what it was that I was going after. I did not like operating that way, but there was no alternative. I had no real line of attack. There was no handle on this one. I had determined, therefore, to simply amass as much information as I could as quickly as possible. Speed always seems particularly essential when I have no idea what it is that might be growing cold.

Andros enlarged before me. I took my bearings from the place where we had eaten the previous evening, then sought the mouth of the stream Vallons had sketched for me.

It took me about ten minutes to locate it, and I throttled down and made my way slowly up its twisting course. Occasionally, I caught a glimpse of a rough roadway running along the bank to my left. The foliage grew denser, however, and I finally lost sight of it completely. Eventually, the boughs met overhead, locking me for several minutes into an alley of premature twilight, before the stream widened again, took me around a corner, and showed me the place as it had been described.

I headed to the pier, where several other boats were moored, tied up, climbed out, and looked around. The building to my right—the only building, outside of a small shed—did extend out over the water, was a wood-frame job, and was so patched that I doubted any of its original materials remained. There were half a dozen vehicles parked beside it, and a faded sign named the place THE CHICKCHARNY. Looking to my left as I advanced, I could see that the road which had accompanied me was in better shape than I would have guessed.

Entering, I discovered a beautiful mahogany bar about fifteen feet ahead of me, looking as if it might have come from some ship. There were eight or ten tables here and there, several of them occupied, and a curtained doorway lay to the right of the bar. Someone had painted a crude halo of clouds above it.

I moved up to the bar, becoming its only occupant. The bartender, a fat man who had needed a shave yesterday as well as the day before, put down his newspaper and came over.

"What'll it be?"

"Give me a beer," I said. "And can I get something to eat?"

"Wait a minute."

He moved farther down, checked a small refrigerator. "Fish-salad sandwich?" he said.

"Okay."

"Good. Because that's all we've got."

He put it together, brought it over, drew me my beer. "That was your boat I heard, wasn't it?" he asked.

"That's right."

"Vacationing?"

"No. I just started work over at Station One."

"Oh. Diver?"

"Yes."

He sighed.

"You're Mike Thornley's replacement, then. Poor guy."

I prefer the word "successor" to "replacement" in these situations, because it makes people seem less like spark plugs. But I nodded.

"Yeah, I heard all about it," I said. "Too bad."

"He used to come here a lot."

"I heard that, too—and that the guy he was with worked here."

He nodded.

"Rudy. Rudy Myers," he said. "Worked here a couple years."

"They were pretty good friends, huh?"

He shook his head.

"Not especially," he said. "They just knew each other. —Rudy worked in back." He glanced at the curtain.

"You know."

I nodded.

"Chief guide, high medical officer, and head bottle washer," he said, with rehearsed levity. "You interested . . . ?"

"What's the specialty of the house?"

"Pink Paradise," he said. "It's nice."

"What's it got?"

"Bit of a drift, bit of an up, the pretty lights."

"Maybe next time," I said. "Did he and Rudy go swimming together often?"

"No, that was the only time. —You worried?"

"I am not exactly happy about it. When I took this job nobody told me I might get eaten. Did Mike ever say anything about unusual marine activity or anything like that?"

"No, not that I can recall."

"What about Rudy? Did he like the water?"

He peered at me, working at the beginnings of a frown.

"Why do you ask?"

"Because it occurs to me that it might make a difference. If he was interested in things like that and Mike came across something unusual, he might take him out to see it."

"Like what?"

"Beats the hell out of me. —But if he found something and it was dangerous, I'd like to know about it."

The frown went away.

"No," he said. "Rudy wouldn't have been interested. He wouldn't have walked outside to look if the Loch Ness monster was swimming by."

"Wonder why he went, then?"

He shrugged.

"I have no idea."

I had a hunch that if I asked him anything else I just might ruin our beautiful rapport. So I ate up, drank up, paid up, and left.

I followed the stream out to the open water again and ran south along the coast. Deems had said it was about four miles that way, figuring from the restaurant, and that it was a long, low building right on the water. All right. I hoped she had returned for that trip Don had mentioned. The worst she could do was tell me to go away. But she knew an awful lot that might be worth hearing. She knew the area and she knew dolphins. I wanted her opinion, if she had one.

There was still a lot of daylight left in the sky, though the air seemed to have cooled a bit, when I spotted a small cove at about the proper distance, throttled down, and swung toward it. Yes, there was the place, partway back and to the left, built against a steep rise and sporting a front deck that projected out over the water. Several boats, one of them a sailboat, rode at rest at its side, sheltered by the long, white curve of a breakwater.

I headed in, continuing to slow, and made my way around the inward point of the breakwall. I saw her sitting on the pier, and she saw me and reached for something. Then she was lost to sight above me as I pulled into the lee of the structure. I killed my engine and tied up to the handiest piling, wondering each moment whether she would appear the next, boathook in hand, ready to repel invaders.

This did not happen, though, so I climbed out and onto a ramplike staging that led me topside. She was just finishing adjusting a long, flaring skirt, which must have been what she had been reaching after. She wore a bikini top, and she was seated on the deck itself, near to the edge, legs tucked out of sight beneath the green, white and blue print material. Her hair was long and very black, her eyes dark and large. Her features were regular, with a definite Oriental cast to them, of the sort I find exceedingly attractive. I paused at the top of the ramp, feeling immediately uncomfortable as I met her gaze.

"My name is Madison, James Madison," I said. "I work out at Station One. I'm new there. May I come up for a minute?"

"You already have," she said. Then she smiled, a tentative thing. "But you can come the rest of the way over and have your minute."

So I did, and as I advanced she kept staring at me. It made me acutely self-conscious, a condition I thought I had mastered shortly after puberty, and as I was about to look away, she said, "Martha Millay—just to make it a full introduction," and she smiled again.

"I've admired your work for a long while," I said, "although that is only part of the reason I came by. I hoped you could help me to feel safer in my own work."

"The killings," she said.

"Yes, Exactly. —Your opinion. I'd like it."

"All right. You can have it," she said. "But I was on Martinique at the time the killings occurred, and my intelligence comes only from the news reports and one phone conversation with a friend at the IDS. On the basis of years of acquaintanceship, years spent photographing them, playing with them, knowing them—loving them —I do not believe it possible that a dolphin would kill a human being. The notion runs contrary to all my experience. For some peculiar reason—perhaps some delphinic concept as to the brotherhood of self-conscious intelligence—we seem to be quite important to them, so important that I even believe one of them might rather die himself than see one of us killed."

"So you would rule out even a self-defense killing by a dolphin?"

"I think so," she said, "although I have no facts to point at here. However, what is more important, in terms of your real question, is that they struck me as very undolphinlike killings."

"How so?"

"I don't see a dolphin as using his teeth in the way that was described. The way a dolphin is designed, his rostrum—or beak—contains a hundred teeth, and there are eighty-eight in his lower jaw. But if he gets into a fight with, say, a shark or a whale, he does not use them for purposes of biting or slashing. He locks them together, which provides a very rigid structure, and uses his lower jaw, which is considerably undershot, for purposes of ramming his opponent. The anterior of the skull is quite thick and the skull itself sufficiently large to absorb enormous shocks from blows administered in this fashion—and they are tremendous blows, for dolphins have very powerful neck muscles. They are quite capable of killing sharks by battering them to death. So even granting for the sake of argument that a dolphin might have done such a thing, he would not have bitten his victims. He would have bludgeoned them."

"So why didn't someone from the dolphin institute come out and say that?"

She sighed.

"They did. The news media didn't even use the statement they gave them. Apparently nobody thought it an important enough story to warrant any sort of followup."

She finally took her eyes off me and stared out over the water.

Then, "I believe their indifference to the damage caused by running only the one story is more contemptible even than actual malice," she finally said.

Acquitted for a moment by her gaze, I lowered myself to sit on the edge of the pier, my feet hanging down over the side. It had been an added discomfort to stand, staring down at her. I joined her in looking out across her harbor.

"Cigarette?" I said.

"I don't smoke."

"Mind if I do?"

"Go ahead."

I lit one, drew on it, thought a moment, then asked, "Any idea as to how the deaths might have occurred?"

"It could have been a shark."

"But there hasn't been a shark in the area for years. The 'walls'—"

She laughed.

"There are any number of ways a shark could have gotten in," she said. "A shift on the bottom, opening a tunnel or crevice beneath the 'wall.' A temporary short circuit in one of the projectors that didn't get noticed— or a continuing one, with a short somewhere in the monitoring system. For that matter, the frequencies used in the 'wall' are supposed to be extremely distressing to many varieties of marine life, but not necessarily fatal. While a shark would normally seek to avoid the 'wall,' one could have been driven, forced through by some disturbance, and then found itself trapped inside."

"That's a thought," I said. "Yes. —Thank you. You didn't disappoint me."

"I would have thought that I had."

"Why?"

"All that I have done is try to vindicate the dolphins and show that there is possibly a shark inside. You said that you wanted me to tell you something that would make you feel safer in your work."

I felt uncomfortable again. I had the sudden, irrational feeling that she somehow knew all about me and was playing games at that moment.

"You said that you are familiar with my work," she said suddenly. "Does that include the two picture books on dolphins?"

"Yes. I enjoyed your text, too."

"There wasn't that much of it," she said, "and it has been several years now. Perhaps it was too whimsical. It has been a long while since I've looked at the things I said. . . ."

"I thought them admirably suited to the subject—little Zen-like aphorisms for each photograph."

"Can you recall any?"

"Yes," I said, one suddenly coming to me, "I remember the shot of the leaping dolphin, where you caught his shadow over the water and had for a caption, 'In the absence of reflection, what gods . . .' "

She chuckled briefly.

"For a long while I thought that that one was perhaps *too* cute. Later, though, as I got to know my subject better, I decided that it was not."

"I have often wondered as to what sort of religion or religious feelings they might possess," I said. "It has been a common element among all the tribes of man. It would seem that something along these lines appears whenever a certain level of intelligence is achieved, for purposes of dealing with those things that are still beyond its grasp. I am baffled as to the forms it might take among dolphins, but quite intrigued by the notion. You say you have some ideas on it?"

"I have done a lot of thinking as I watched them," she said, "attempting to analyze their character in terms of their behavior, their physiology. Are you familiar with the writings of Johan Huizinga?"

"Faintly," I said. "It has been years since I read *Homo Ludens,* and it struck me as a rough draft for something he never got to work out completely. But I recall his basic premise as being that culture begins as a sort of sublimation of a play instinct, elements of sacred performances and festal contests continuing for a time in the evolving institutions, perhaps always remaining present at some level—although his analysis stopped short of modern times."

"Yes," she said. "The play instinct. Watching them sport about, it has often seemed to me that as well adapted as they are to their environment, there was never a need for dolphins to evolve complex social institutions, so that whatever it was they did possess along those lines was much closer to the earlier situations considered by Huizinga—a life condition filled with an overt indulgence in their version of festal performances and contests."

"A play-religion?"

"Not quite that simple, though I think that is part of the picture. The problem here lies in language. Huizinga employed the Latin word *ludus* for a reason. Unlike the Greek language, which had a variety of words for idling, for competing in contests, for passing the time in different fashions, Latin reflected the basic unity of all these things and summarized them into a single concept by means of the word *ludus*. The dolphins' distinctions between play and seriousness are obviously different from our own, just as ours are different from the Greeks'. In our understanding of the meaning of *ludus*, however, in our ability to realize that we may unify instances of activity from across a broad spectrum of behavior patterns by considering them as a form of play, we have a better basis for conjecture as well as interpretation."

"And in this manner you have deduced their religion?"

"I haven't, of course. I only have a few conjectures. You say you have none?"

"Well, if I had to guess, just to pull something out of the air, I would say some form of pantheism—perhaps something akin to the less contemplative forms of Buddhism."

"Why 'less contemplative'?" she asked.

"All that activity," I said. "They don't even really sleep, do they? They have to get topside quite regularly in order to breathe. So they are always moving about. When would they be able to drift beneath the coral equivalent of a bo tree for any period of time?"

"What do you think your mind would be like if you never slept?"

"I find that rather difficult to conceive. But I imagine I would find it quite distressing after a while, unless . . ."

"Unless what?"

"Unless I indulged in periodic daydreaming, I suppose."

"I think that might be the case with dolphins, although with a brain capacity such as they possess I do not feel it need necessarily be a periodic thing."

"I don't quite follow you."

"I think they are sufficiently endowed to do it simultaneously with other thinking, rather than serially."

"You mean always dreaming a little? Taking their mental vacations, their reveries, sidewise in time as it were?"

"Yes. We do it too, to a limited extent. There is always a little background thinking, a little mental noise going on while we are dealing with whatever thoughts are most pressing in our consciousness. We learn to suppress it, calling this concentration. It is, in one sense, a process of keeping ourselves from dreaming."

"And you see the dolphin as dreaming and carrying on his normal mental business at the same time?"

"In a way, yes. But I also see the dreaming itself as a somewhat different process."

"In what way?"

"Our dreams are largely visual in nature, for our waking lives are primarily visually oriented. The dolphin, on the other hand—"

"—is acoustically oriented. Yes. Granting this constant dreaming effect and predicating it on the neurophysiological structures they possess, it would seem that they might splash around enjoying their own sound tracks."

"More or less, yes. And might not this behavior come under the heading of *ludus?*"

"I just don't know."

"One form of *ludus*, which the Greeks of course saw as a separate activity, giving it the name *diagoge,* is best translated as mental recreation. Music was placed in this category, and Aristotle speculated in his *Politics* as to the profit to be derived from it, finally conceding that music might conduce to virtue by making the body fit, promoting a certain ethos, and enabling us to enjoy things in the proper way—whatever that means. But considering an accoustical daydream in this light—as a musical variety of *ludus*—I wonder if it might not indeed promote a certain ethos and foster a particular way of enjoying things?"

"Possibly, if they were shared experiences."

"We still have no proper idea as to the meanings of many of their sounds. Supposing they are vocalizing some part of this experience?"

"Perhaps, given your other premises."

"Then that is all I have," she said. "I choose to see a religious significance in spontaneous expressions of *diagoge*. You may not."

"I don't. I'd buy it as a physiological or psychological necessity, even see it—as you suggested—as a form of play, or *ludus*. But I have no way of knowing whether such musical activity is truly a religious expression, so for me the ball stops rolling right there. At this point, we do not really understand their ethos or their particular ways of viewing life. A concept as alien and sophisticated as the one you have outlined would be well-nigh impossible for them to communicate to us, even if the language barrier were a lot thinner than it is now. Short of actually finding a way of getting inside them to know it for oneself, I do not see how we can deduce religious sentiments here, even if every one of your other conjectures is correct."

"You are, of course, right," she said. "The conclusion is not scientific if it cannot be demonstrated. I cannot demonstrate it, for it is only a feeling, an inference, an intuition—and I offer it only in that spirit. But watch them at their play sometime, listen to the sounds your ears will accept. Think about it. Try to feel it."

I continued to stare at the water and the sky. I had already learned everything I had come to find out and the rest was just frosting, but I did not have the pleasure of such desserts every day. I realized then that I liked the girl even more than I had thought I would, that I had grown quite fascinated as she had spoken, and not entirely because of the subject. So, partly to prolong things and partly because I was genuinely curious, I said, "Go ahead. Tell me the rest. Please."

"The rest?"

"You see a religion or something on that order. Tell me what you think it must be like."

She hesitated. Then, "I don't know," she said. "The more one compounds conjectures the sillier one becomes. Let us leave it at that."

But that would leave me with little to say but "Thank you" and "Good night." So I pushed my mind around inside the parameters she had laid down, and one of the things that came to me was Barthelme's mention of the normal distribution curve with reference to dolphins.

"If, as you suggest," I began, "they constantly express and interpret themselves and their universe by a kind of subliminal dreamsong, it would seem to follow that, as in all things, some are better at it than others. How many Mozarts can there be, even in a race of musicians? Champions, in a nation of athletes? If they all play at a religious *diagoge*, it must follow that some are superior players. Would they be priests or prophets? Bards? Holy singers? Would the areas in which they dwell be shrines, holy places? A dolphin Vatican or Mecca? A Lourdes?"

She laughed.

"Now *you* are getting carried away, Mister—Madison."

I looked at her, trying to see something beyond the apparently amused expression with which she faced me.

"You told me to think about it," I said; "to try to feel it."

"It would be strange if you were correct, would it not?"

I nodded.

"And probably well worth the pilgrimage," I said, standing, "if only I could find an interpreter. —I thank you for the minute I took and the others you gave me.

Would you mind terribly if I dropped by again sometime?"

"I am afraid I am going to be quite busy," she said.

"I see. Well, I appreciate what you have given me.
Good night, then."

"Good night."

I made my way back down the ramp to the speedboat, brought it to life, guided it about the breakwall
and headed toward the darkening sea, looking back only
once, in hopes of discovering just what it was that she
called to mind, sitting there, looking out across the
waves. Perhaps the Little Mermaid, I decided.

She did not wave back to me. But then it was twilight,
and she might not have noticed.

Returning to Station One, I felt sufficiently inspired to
head for the office/museum/library cluster to see what I
could pick up in the way of reading materials having to
do with dolphins.

I made my way across the islet and into the front
door, passing the shadow-decked models and displays of
the museum and turning right. I swung the door open.
The light was on in the library, but the place was empty.
I found several books listed that I had not read, so I
hunted them up, leafed through them, settled on two,
and went to sign them out.

As I was doing this, my eyes were drawn toward the
top of the ledger page by one of the names entered
there: Mike Thornley. I glanced across at the date and
saw that it happened to be the day before his death. I finished signing out my own materials and decided to see
what it was he had taken to read on the eve of his passing. Well, read and listen to. There were three items
shown, and the prefix to one of the numbers indicated
that it had been a tape.

The two books turned out to be light popular novels.
When I checked the tape, however, a very strange feeling possessed me. It was not music, but rather one from

the marine-biology section. Verily. To be precise, it was
a recording of the sounds of the killer whale.

Even my pedestrian knowledge of the subject was sufficient, but to be doubly certain, I checked in one of the
books I had right there with me. Yes, the killer whale
was undoubtedly the dolphin's greatest enemy, and well
over a generation ago experiments had been conducted
at the Naval Undersea Center in San Diego, using the
recorded sounds of the killer whale to frighten dolphins,
for purposes of developing a device to scare them out of
tuna nets, where they were often inadvertently slaugh-
tered.

What could Thornley possibly have wanted it for? Its
use in a waterproof broadcasting unit could well have
accounted for the unusual behavior of the dolphins in
the park at the time he was killed. But why? Why do a
thing like that?

I did what I always do when I am puzzled: I sat
down and lit a cigarette.

While this made it even more obvious to me that
things were not what they had seemed at the time of the
killings, it also caused me once again to consider the apparent nature of the attack. I thought of the photos I
had seen of the bodies, of the medical reports I had
read.

Bitten. Chewed. Slashed.

Arterial bleeding, right carotid . . .

Severed jugular; numerous lacerations of shoulders
and chest . . .

According to Martha Millay, a dolphin would not go
about it that way. Still, as I recalled, their many teeth,
while not enormous, were needle-sharp. I began paging
through the books, looking for photographs of the jaws
and teeth.

Then the thought came to me, with dark, more than
informational overtones to it: *there is a dolphin skeleton
in the next room.*

Mashing out my cigarette, I rose then, passed through

the doorway into the museum, and began looking about for the light switch. It was not readily apparent. As I sought it, I heard the door on the other side of the room open.

Turning, I saw Linda Cashel stepping across the threshold. With her next step, she looked in my direction, froze, and muffled the beginning of a shriek.

"It's me. Madison," I said. "Sorry I alarmed you. I'm looking for the light switch."

Several seconds passed. Then, "Oh," she said. "It's down in back of the display. I'll show you."

She crossed to the front door, groped behind a component model.

The lights came on, and she gave a nervous laugh.

"You startled me," she said. "I was working late. An unusual thing, but I got backed up. I stepped out for a breath of air and didn't see you come in."

"I've got the books I was looking for," I said, "but thanks for finding me the switch."

"I'll be glad to sign them out for you."

"I already did that," I said, "but I left them inside because I wanted to take another look at the display before I went home."

"Oh. Well, I was just going to close up. If you want to stay awhile, I'll let you do it."

"What does it consist of?"

"Just turning out the lights and closing the doors—we don't lock them around here. I've already shut the windows."

"Sure, I'll do that. —I'm sorry I frightened you."

"That's all right. No harm done."

She moved to the front door, turned when she reached it, and smiled again, a better job this time.

"Well, good night."

"Good night."

My first thought was that there were no signs of any extra work having come in since the last time I had been around, my second one was that she had been trying a little too hard to get me to believe her, and my third thought was ignoble.

But the proof of the pudding would keep. I turned my attention to the dolphin skeleton.

The lower jaw, with its neat, sharp teeth, fascinated me, and its size came close to being its most interesting feature. Almost, but not quite. The most interesting thing about it had to be the fact that the wires which held it in place were clean, untarnished, bright and gleaming at their ends, as if they had just recently been cut—unlike their more oxidized brethren everyplace else where the specimen had been wired.

The thing I found interesting about the size was that it was just about right to make it a dandy hand weapon.

And that was all. That was enough. But I fingered the maxillary and premaxillary bones, running my hand back toward the blowhole; I traced the rostrum; I gripped the jaw once more. Why, I did not really know for a moment, until a grotesque vision of Hamlet filtered into my mind. Or was it really that incongruous? A phrase out of Loren Eiseley came to me then: ". . .We are all potential fossils still carrying within our bodies the crudities of former existences, the marks of a world in which living creatures flow with little more consistency than clouds from age to age." We came from the water. This fellow I gripped had spent his life there. But both our skulls were built of calcium, a sea product chosen in our earlier days and irrevocably part of us now; both were housings for large brains—similar, yet different; both seemed to contain a center of consciousness, awareness, sensitivity, with all the concomitant pleasures, woes, and available varieties of conclusions concerning existence which that entailed, passing at some time or other within these small, rigid pieces of carbonate of lime. The only really significant difference, I suddenly felt, was not that this fellow had been born a dolphin and I a man, but only, rather, that I still lived—a very minor point in terms of the time scale onto which I had wandered. I withdrew my hand, wondering uncomfortably whether my remains would ever be used as a murder weapon.

Having no further reason for being there, I collected my books, closed up, and cleared out.

Returning to my cottage, I deposited the books on my bed table and left the small light burning there. I departed again by means of the back door, which let upon a small, relatively private patio, pleasantly situated right at the edge of the islet with an unobstructed view of the sea. But I did not pause to admire the prospect just then. If other people might step out for a breath of air, so could I.

I strolled until I located a suitable spot, a small bench in the shadow of the dispensary. I seated myself there, fairly well hidden, yet commanding a full view of the complex I had but recently quitted. For a long while I waited, feeling ignoble, but watching anyway.

As the minutes continued their parade, I came near to deciding that I had been mistaken, that the margin of caution had elapsed, that nothing would occur.

But then the door at the far end of the office—the one through which I had entered on my initial tour of the place—opened, and the figure of a man emerged. He headed toward the nearest shore of the islet, then commenced what would have seemed but the continuance of a stroll along its edge to anyone just noticing him there. He was tall, around my height, which narrowed the field considerably, so that it was really almost unnecessary for me to wait and see him enter the cottage that was assigned to Paul Vallons, and after a moment see the light go on within.

A little while later, I was in bed with my dolphin books, reflecting that some guys seem to have it made all the way around; and puzzling and wondering, with the pied typecase Don had handed me, that I was ever born to set it right.

The following morning, during the ambulatory, coffee-tropism phase of preconsciousness, I stumbled across the most damnable, frightening item in the entire case. Or rather, I stepped over it—perhaps even on it —before its existence registered itself. There followed an appreciable time lag, and then its possible significance occurred to me.

I stooped and picked it up: an oblong of stiff paper, an envelope, which had apparently been pushed in beneath the back door. At least, it lay near to it.

I took it with me to the kitchenette table, tore it open, extracted and unfolded the paper it contained. Sipping my coffee, I read over the block-printed message several times:

AFFIXED TO THE MAINMAST OF THE WRECK, ABOUT A FOOT BENEATH THE MUD

That was all. That was it.

But I was suddenly fully awake. It was not just the message, as intriguing as I naturally found it, but the fact that someone had selected me as its recipient. Who? And why?

Whatever it was—and I was certain there was something—I was most disturbed by the implication that someone was aware of my extraordinary reasons for being there, with the necessary corollary that that person knew too much about me. My hackles rose, and the adrenaline tingles came into my extremities. No man knew my name; a knowledge of it jeopardized my existence. In the past, I had even killed to protect my identity.

My first impulse was to flee, to throw over the case, dispose of this identity and lose myself in the manner in which I had become adept. But then I would never know, would never know when, where, how, why, and in what fashion I had been tripped up, found out. And most important, by whom.

Also, considering the message again, I had no assurance that flight would be the end of things for me. For was there not an element of coercion here? Of tacit blackmail in the implied imperative? It was as if the sender were saying, *I know. I will assist. I will keep silent. For there is a thing you will do for me.*

Of course I would go and inspect the wreck, though I would have to wait until the day's work was done. No use speculating as to what I would find, although I would handle it most gingerly. That gave me the entire day in which to consider what I might have done wrong, and to decide upon the best means of defending myself. I rubbed my ring, where the death spores slept, then rose and went to shave.

Paul and I were sent over to Station Five that day. Standard inspection and maintenance work. Dull, safe, routine. We scarcely got wet.

He gave no indication of knowing that I was on to anything. In fact, he even started several conversations. In one, he asked me, "Did you get over to the Chick-charny?"

"Yes," I said.

"What did you think of it?"

"You were right. A dive."

He smiled and nodded. then, "Try any of their specialities?" he asked.

"Just had a few beers."

"That was safest," he said. "Mike—my friend who died—used to go there a lot."

"Oh?"

"I used to go with him at first. He'd take something and I'd sit around and drink and wait for him to come down."

"You didn't go in for it yourself?"

He shook his head.

"Had a bad experience when I was younger. Scared me. Anyway, so did he—there, I mean—several times, at the Chickcharny. He used to go in back—it's a sort of ashram back there. Did you see it?"

"No."

"Well, he had a couple bad ones in there and we got in an argument about it. He knew the damn place wasn't licensed, but he didn't care. I finally told him he ought to keep a safe supply at the station, but he was worried about the damn company regulations against it. Which I think was silly. Anyhow, I finally told him he could go by himself if he wanted to go that badly and couldn't wait till the weekend to go someplace else. I stopped going."

"Did he?"

"Only recently," he said. "The hard way."

"Oh."

"So if you do go in for it, I'm telling you the same thing I told him: Keep your own around if you can't wait to go someplace farther and cleaner than that."

"I'll remember," I said, wondering then whether he might, perhaps, be on to something about me and be encouraging my breaking the company rules for purposes of getting rid of me. That seemed kind of far-out, though, a little too paranoiac a reaction on my part. So I dismissed it.

"Did he have any more bad ones?" I asked.

"I think so," he said. "I don't really know."

And that was all he had to say on the subject. I wanted to ask him more things, of course, but our acquaintanceship was still such that I knew I would need an opening to get through, and he didn't give me any.

So we finished up, returned to Station One, went our separate ways. I stopped by and told Davies I wanted a boat later. He assigned me one, and I returned to my cottage and waited until I saw him leave for dinner. Then I want back to the docks, threw my diving gear into the boat, and took off. This elaboration was necessary because of the fact that solo-diving was against the rules, and also because of the safety precautions Barthelme and enunciated to me that first day. —True, they applied only inside the area and the ship lay outside it, but I did not care to explain where I was going either.

The thought had of course occurred to me that it might be a trap, set to spring in any of a number of ways. While I hoped my friend in the museum still had his lower jaw in place, I did not discount the possibility of an underwater ambush. In fact, I had one of the little death rods along with me, all loaded and primed. The photos had been quite clear. I did not forget. Nor did I discount the possibility of a booby trap. I would simply have to be very careful in my poking about.

While I did not know what would happen if I were spotted solo-diving with company gear, I would have to count on my ability to talk or lie my way out of it, if catching me in this breach of domestic tranquillity was what the note's author had had in mind.

I came to what I thought to be the spot, anchored there, slipped into my gear, went over the side and down.

The cool smoothness held me and I did my dance of descent, curious, wary, with a heightened feeling of fragility. Toward the bottom then, with steady, sweeping movements down, I passed from cool to cold and light to dark. I switched on my torch, shot the beam about.

Minutes later, I found it, circled it, hunting about the vicinity for signs of fellow intruders.

But no, nothing. I seemed to be alone.

I made my way toward the hulk then, casting my light down the splintered length of the short-snapped mainmast. Small fish appeared, staging an unruly demonstration in the neighborhood of the gunwale. My light fell upon the layer of ooze at the base of the mast. It appeared undisturbed, but then I have no idea as to how long it takes ooze to settle.

Coming up beside/above it then, I probed it with a thin rod I had brought along. After several moments, I was satisfied that there was a small, oblong object, probably metallic, about eight inches beneath the surface.

Drawing nearer, I scooped away a layer. The water muddied, fresh material moving to fill the site of my excavation. Cursing mentally, I extended my left hand, fingers at full flex, slowly, carefully, down into the mud.

I encountered no obstacles until I reached the box itself. No wires, strings, foreign objects. It was definitely metal, and I traced its outline: about six by ten by three inches. It was upended and held in place against the mast by a double strand of wire. I felt no connections with anything else, so I uncovered it—at least momentarily—for a better look.

It was a small, standard looking strongbox, handles on both ends and on the top. The wires ran through two of these loops. I shook out a coil of plastic cord and knotted it through the nearest one. After paying out a considerable length of it, I leaned down and used the pliers I had carried with me to sever the wires that held the box to the mast. Upward then, playing out the rest of the line behind me.

Back in the boat and out of my gear, I hauled it, hand over hand, up from the depths. The movement, the pressure changes did not serve to set anything off, so I felt a little safer in handling it when I finally brought it aboard. I set it on the deck and thought about it as I unfastened and recoiled the line.

The box was locked, and whatever was inside shifted around when I moved it. I sprung the lock with a screwdriver. Then I went over the side into the water, and holding on, reaching from there, I used the rod to flip back the lid.

But for the lapping of the waves and the sounds of my breathing, there was silence. So I reboarded and took a look inside.

It contained a canvas bag with a fold-down flap that snapped closed. I unsnapped it.

Stones. It was filled with dozens of rather undistinguished-looking stones. But since people generally have a reason for going to that much trouble, there had to be a decent intrinsic value involved. I dried off several of them, rubbing them vigorously with my towel. Then I turned them around every which way. Yes, there were a few glints, here and there.

I had not been lying to Cashel when he had asked what I knew about minerals and I had said, "A little." Only a little. But in this instance it seemed that it might be enough. Selecting the most promising specimen for the experiment, I chipped away at the dirty minerals that sheathed the stone. Several minutes later, an edge of the material I had exposed exhibited great scratching abilities with the various materials on which I tested it.

Someone was smuggling diamonds and someone else wanted me to know about it. What did my informant expect me to do with this information? Obviously, if he had simply wanted the authorities informed he would have done it himself.

Knowing that I was being used for purposes I did not yet understand, I decided to do what was probably expected of me, inasmuch as it coincided with what I would have done anyhow.

I was able to dock and unload the gear without encountering any problems. I kept the bag of stones wrapped in my towel until I was back in my cottage. No more messages had been slipped beneath the door. I repaired to the shower stall and cleaned myself up.

I couldn't think of anyplace really clever to hide the stones, so I stuffed the bag down into the garbage-disposal unit and replaced the drain cover. That would have to do. Before stashing it, though, I removed four of the ugly ducklings. Then I dressed and took a walk.

Strolling near, I saw that Frank and Linda were eating out on their patio, so I returned to my place and made myself a quick, prefabricated meal. Afterward, I watched the sun in its descending for perhaps twenty minutes. Then, what seemed an adequate period having passed, I made my way back again.

It was even better than I had hoped for. Frank sat alone, reading, on the now-cleared patio. I moved up and said, "Hello."

He turned toward me, smiled, nodded, lowered his book.

"Hello, Jim," he said. "Now that you've been here a few days, how do you like it?"

"Oh, fine," I said. "Just fine. How is everything with you?"

He shrugged.

"Can't complain. — We were going to ask you over to dinner. Perhaps tomorrow?"

"Sounds great. Thanks."

"Come by about six?"

"All right."

"Have you found any interesting diversions yet?"

"Yes. As a matter of fact, I took your advice and resurrected my old rock-hounding habits."

"Oh? Come across any interesting specimens?"

"It just happens that I did," I said. "It was really an amazing accident. I doubt whether anybody would have located them except by accident. Here. I'll show you."

I dug them out of my pocket and dumped them into his hand.

He stared. He fingered them. He shifted them around. For perhaps half a minute.

Then, "You want to know what they are, is that it?" he asked.

"No. I already know that."

"I see."

He looked at me and smiled.

"Where did you find them?"

I smiled, very slowly.

"Are there more?" he asked.

I nodded.

He moistened his lips. He returned the stones.

"Well, tell me this, if you will—what sort of deposit was it?"

Then I thought faster than I had at any time since my arrival. It was something about the way he had asked it that put my mind to spinning. I had been thinking purely in terms of a diamond-smuggling operation, with him as the natural disposer of the contraband stones. Now, though, I reviewed what scanty knowledge I did possess on the subject. The largest mines in the world were those of South Africa, where diamonds were found embedded in that rock known as kimberlite, or "blue ground." But how did they get there in the first place? Through volcanic action—as bits of carbon that had been trapped in streams of molten lava, subjected to intense heat and pressure that altered their structure to the hard, crystalline form of a girl's best friend. But there were also alluvial deposits—diamonds that had been cut free from their resting places by the actions of ancient streams, often borne great distances from their points of origin, and accumulated in offshore pockets. That was Africa, of course, and while I did not know much offhand as to New World deposits, much of the Caribbean island system had been built up by means of volcanic activity. The possibility of local deposits—of the volcanic-pipe variety or alluvial—was not precluded.

In view of my somewhat restricted area for activity since my arrival, I said, "Alluvial. It wasn't a pipe, I'll tell you that."

He nodded.

"Have you any idea as to the extent of your find?" he inquired.

"Not really," I said. "There are more where these came from. But as to the full extent of their distribution, it is simply too early for me to tell."

"Most interesting," he said. "You know, it jibes with a notion I've long held concerning this part of the world. You wouldn't care to give me just a very rough, general sort of idea as to what part of the ocean these are from, would you?"

"Sorry," I said. "You understand."

"Of course, of course. Still, how far would you go from here for an afternoon's adventure?"

"I suppose that would depend on my own notions on this matter—as well as available air transportation, or hydrofoil."

He smiled.

"All right. I won't press you any further. But I'm curious. Now that you've got them, what are you going to do with them?"

I took my time lighting a cigarette.

"Get as much as I can for them and keep my mouth shut, of course," I finally said.

He nodded.

"Where are you going to sell them? Stop passersby on the street?"

"I don't know," I said. "I haven't thought that much about it yet. I suppose I could take them to some jeweler's."

He chuckled.

"If you're very lucky. If you're lucky, you'll find one willing to take a chance. If you're very lucky, you'll find one willing to take a chance and also willing to give you a fair deal. I assume you would like to avoid the creation of a record, the crediting of extra income to your master account? Taxable income?"

"As I said, I would like to get as much as I can for them."

"Naturally. Then am I correct in assuming that your purpose in coming to me over this might somehow be connected with this desire?"

"In a word, yes."

"I see."

"Well?"

"I am thinking. To act as your agent for something like this would not be without risks of its own."

"How much?"

"No, I'm sorry," he said then. "It is probably too risky altogether. After all, it is illegal. I'm a married man. I could jeopardize my job by getting involved in something like this. If it had come along perhaps fifteen years ago . . . well, who knows? I'm sorry. Your secret is safe. Don't worry about that. But I would just as soon not be party to the enterprise."

"You are certain of that?"

"Positive. The return would have to be quite high for me even to consider it."

"Twenty percent?" I said.

"Out of the question."

"Maybe twenty-five . . . " I said.

"No. Twice that would scarcely—"

"Fifty percent? You're crazy!"

"Please! Keep your voice down! You want the whole station to hear?"

"Sorry. But that's out of the question. Fifty percent! No. If I can find a willing jeweler. I'll still be better off —even if he does cheat me. Twenty-five percent is tops. Absolutely."

"I am afraid I can't see it."

"Well, I wish you would think about it anyway."

He chuckled.

"It will be difficult to forget," he said.

"Okay. —Well, I'll be seeing you."

"Tomorrow, at six."

"Right. Good night."

"Good night."

So I began walking back, reflecting on the possible permutations of people and events leading up to and culminating in the killings. But there were still too many gaps in the picture for me to come up with anything I really liked.

I was most troubled, of course, by the fact that there was someone who was aware that my presence actually represented more than its outward appearance. I searched my mind again and again for possible giveaways, but I did not see where I could have slipped up. I had been quite careful about my credentials. I had encountered no one with whom I had ever been familiar. I began wishing, not for the first time—nor, I was certain, the last—that I had not accepted this case.

I considered then what I ought to be about next, to push the investigation further along. I supposed I could inspect the place where the bodies had been found. I had not been there yet, mainly because I doubted there would be anything to be learned from it. Still . . . I put that on my list for the morrow, if I could hit it before dinner with the Cashels. If not, then the next day.

I wondered whether I had done the expected thing as to the stones. I felt that I had, and I was very curious as to the repercussions—almost, but not quite, as curious as I was concerning the motives of my informant. Nothing I could do at the moment, though, but wait.

Thinking these thoughts, I heard myself hailed by Andy Deems from where he stood near his cottage, smoking his pipe. He wondered whether I was interested in a game of chess. I wasn't, really, but I went over anyhow. I lost two and managed to stalemate him on the third one. I felt very uncomfortable around him, but at least I didn't have to say much.

The following day, Deems and Carter were sent over to Station Six, while Paul and I took our turn at "miscellaneous duties as assigned" in and about the equipment shed. Another time-marking episode, I had decided, till I got to my real work once more.

And so it went, until late afternoon, when I was beginning to wonder what sort of cook Linda Cashel might be. Barthelme hurried into the shed.

"Get your gear together," he said. "We have to go out."

"What's the matter?" Paul asked him.

"Something is wrong with one of the sonic genera-
tors."

"What?"

He shook his head.

"No way of telling till we've brought it back and
checked it over. All I know is that a light's gone out on
the board. I want to pull the whole package and put in a
new unit. No attempt at underwater repair work on this
one, even if it looks simple. I want to go over it very
carefully in the lab."

"Where is it situated?"

"To the southwest, at about twenty-eight fathoms. Go
look at the board if you want. It will give you a better
picture. —But don't take too long, all right? There are a
lot of things to load."

"Right. Which vessel?"

"The *Mary Ann.*"

"The new deepwater rules . . . ?"

"Yes. Load everything. I'm going down to tell Davies
now. Then I'm going to change clothes. I'll be back
shortly."

"See you then."

"Yes."

He moved away and we set to work, getting our own
gear, the shark cage, and the submersible decompression
chamber ready to go. We made two trips to the *Mary
Ann,* then took a break to go see the map, learned nothing new from it, and returned for the DC, which was
stored on a cart.

"Ever been down in that area before?" I asked Paul
as we began maneuvering the cart along.

"Yes," he said. "Some time back. It is fairly near to
the edge of a submarine canyon. That's why there's a
big bite out of that corner of the 'wall.' It plunges pretty
sharply right beyond that section of the perimeter."

"Will that complicate things any?"

"It shouldn't," he said, "unless a whold section broke
loose and carried everything down with it. Then we

would have to anchor and hook up a whole new hous-
ing, instead of just switching the guts. That would take us
somewhat longer. I'll review the work with you on the
unit we'll be taking out."

"Good."

Barthelme rejoined us about then. He and Davies,
who would also be going along, helped get everything
stowed. Twenty minutes later, we were on our way.

The winch was rigged to lower both the shark cage
and the decompression chamber tandem-fashion and in
that order. Paul and I rode the DC down, keeping the
extra lines from tangling, playing our lights about as we
descended. While I had never had to use one, I had always found the presence of a decompression chamber
on the bottom a thing of comfort, despite its slightly om-
inous function for the sort of work we would be doing.
It was good to know that if I were injured I could get inside, signal, and be hauled directly to the top with no
delays for decompression stops, the bottomside pressure
being maintained in the bell's chamber on the way up
and gradually returned to normal as they rushed me
back to the dispensary. A heartening thought for all
that, time-wise.

Bottomside, we positioned the cage near to the unit,
which we found still standing, exhibiting no visible signs
of damage, and we halted the illuminated DC a couple
of fathoms up and off to the east. We were indeed on
the edge of a steep cliff. While Paul inspected the sonic-broadcast unit, I moved nearer and flashed my light
downward.

Jutting rocky pinnacles and twisting crevices . . . Re-
flexively, I drew back from the edge of the abyss, turned
my light away. I returned and watched Paul work.

It took him ten minutes to disconnect the thing and
free it from its mountings. Another five saw it secured
and rising on its lines.

A bit later, in the periodic sweep of our beams, we

caught sight of the replacement unit on the way down. We swam up to meet it and guided it into place. This time, Paul let me go to work. I indicated by pantomime that I wanted to, and he wrote on his slate: GO AHEAD SEE WHAT YOU REMEMB.

So I fastened it in place, and this took me about twenty minutes. He inspected the work, patted me on the shoulder, and nodded. I moved to connect the systems then, but stopped to glance at him. He indicated that I should go ahead.

This only took a few minutes, and when I was finished I had a certain feeling of satisfaction thinking of that light going on again on the big board back at the station. I turned around to indicate that the job was done and that he could come admire my work.

But he was no longer with me.

For a few seconds I froze, startled. Then I began shining my light around.

No, no. Nothing. . . .

Growing somewhat panicky, I moved to the edge of the abyss and swept downward with the light. Luckily, he was not moving very quickly. But he was headed downward, all right. I took off after him as fast as I could move.

Nitrogen narcosis, deepwater sickness, or "rapture of the deep" does not usually hit at depths above 200 feet. Still, we were at around 170, so it was possible, and he certainly seemed to be showing the symptoms.

Worrying then about my own state of mind, I reached him, caught him by the shoulder, turned him back. Through his mask, I could see the blissful expression that he wore.

Taking him by the arm and shoulder, I began drawing him back with me. For several seconds he accompanied me, offering no resistance.

Then he began to struggle. I had anticipated this possibility and shifted my grips into a *kwansetsu-waza* position, but quickly discovered that judo is not exactly the same underwater, especially when a tank valve is too near your mask or mouthpiece. I had to keep twisting my head away, pulling it back. For a time, it became impossible to guide him that way. But I refused to relinquish my grip. If I could just hold him a while longer and did not get hit by narcosis myself, I felt that I had the advantage. After all, his coordination was affected as well as his thinking.

I finally got him to the DC—a wild antenna of bubbles rising from his air hose by then, as he had spat out his mouthpiece and there was no way I could get it back in without letting go. Still, it might have been one of the reasons he became easier to manage near the end there. I don't know.

I stuffed him into the lighted chamber, followed, and got the hatch sealed. He gave up about then and began to sag. I was able to get his mouthpiece back into place, and then I threw the pull-up switch.

We began to rise almost immediately, and I wondered what Barthelme and Davies were thinking at that moment.

They got us up very quickly. I felt a slight jarring as we came to rest on the deck. Shortly afterward, the water was pumped out. I don't know what the pressure was up to—or down to—at that point, but the communicator came alive and I heard Bartheleme's voice as I was getting out of my gear.

"We'll be moving in a few minutes," he said. "What happened, and how serious is it?"

"Nitrogen narcosis, I'd say. Paul just started swimming out and down, struggled with me when I tried to bring him back."

"Was either of you hurt?"

"No, I don't think so. He lost his mouthpiece for a little while. But he's breathing okay now."

"What shape is he in otherwise?"

"Still rapturing, I'd guess. Sort of collapsed, drunken look to him."

"All right. You might as well get out of your gear—"

"I already have."

"—and get him out of his."

"Just starting."

"We'll radio ahead and have a medic hop out and be waiting at the dispensary, just in case. Sounds like what he really needs most is the chamber, though. So we'll just take it slow and easy in getting him back to surface pressure. I'm making an adjustment right now. . . . Do you have any rapture symptoms yourself?"

"No."

"Okay, there. We'll leave it at this setting for a little while. —Is there anything else I should know?"

"Not that I can think of."

"All right, then. I'm going forward to radio for the doctor. If you want me for anything, whistle into the speaker. That should carry."

"Right."

I got Paul out of his rig then, hoping he would start coming around soon. But he didn't.

He just sat there, slouched, mumbling, eyes open but glassy. Every now and then he smiled.

I wondered what was wrong. If the pressure was indeed diminished, the recovery should have been almost instantaneous. Probably needed one more step, I decided.

But—

Could he have been down much earlier that morning, before the workday began?

Decompression time does depend upon the total amount of time spent underwater during about a twelve-hour period, since you are dealing with the total amount of nitrogen absorbed by the tissues, particularly the brain and spinal cord. Might he have been down looking for something, say, in the mud, at the base of a broken mast, amid the wreckage of a certain old vessel? Perhaps down for a long while, searching carefully, worried? Knowing that he had shore duty today, that there should be no more nitrogen accumulated during this workday? Then, suddenly, an emergency, and he has to chance it. He takes it as easy as possible, even encouraging the new man to go ahead and finish up the job. Resting, trying to hang on . . .

It could well be. In which case, Barthelme's decompression values were off. The time is measured from surface to surface, and the depth is reckoned from the deepest point reached in any of the dives. Hell, for all I knew he might have visited several caches spotted at various points along the ocean's bottom.

I leaned over, studied the pupils of his eyes—catching his attention, it seemed, in the process.

"How long were you down this morning?" I asked.

He smiled.

"Wasn't," he said.

"It doesn't matter what was involved. It's your health we're worried about now. —How long were you down? What depths?"

He shook his head.

"Wasn't," he said.

"Damn it! I know you were! It was the old wreck, wasn't it? That's maybe twenty fathoms. So how long? An hour? Were you down more than once?"

"Wasn't down!" he insisted. "Really, Mike! I wasn't."

I sighed, leaned back. Maybe, possibly, he was telling the truth. People are all different inside. Perhaps his physiology was playing some other variation of the game than the one I had guessed at. It had been so neat, though. For a moment, I had seen him as the supplier of the stones and Frank as the fence. Then I had gone to Frank with my find, Frank had mentioned this development to him, and Paul, worried, had gone off while the station slept to make certain that things were still where they were supposed to be. His tissues accumulated a lot of nitrogen during his frantic searching, and then this happened. It certainly struck me as logical. But if it were me, I would have admitted to having been down. I could always come up with some lie as to the reason later.

"Don't you remember?" I tried again.

He commenced an uninspired stream of curses, but lost his enthusiasm before a dozen or so syllables. His voice trailed off, then, "Why don't you b'lieve me, Mike? I wasn't down. . . ."

"All right, I believe you," I said. "It's okay. Just take it easy."

He reached out and took hold of my arm.

"It's all beautiful," he said.

"Yeah."

"Everything is just—like it's never been before."

"What did you take?" I asked him.

". . . Beautiful."

"What are you on?" I insisted.

"You know I never take any," he finally said.

"Then what's causing it, whatever it is? Do you know?"

"Damn fine . . ." he said.

"Something went wrong on the bottom. What was it?"

"I don't know! Go away! Don't bring it back. . . . This is how it should be. Always. . . . Not that crap you take. . . . Started all the trouble . . ."

"I'm sorry," I said.

". . . That started it."

"I know. I'm sorry. Spoiled things," I ventured. "Shouldn't have."

". . . Talked," he said. ". . . Blew it."

"I know. I'm sorry. But we got him," I tried.

"Yeah," he said. Then, "Oh, my God!"

"The diamonds. The diamonds are safe," I suggested quickly.

"Got him. . . . Oh, my God! I'm sorry!"

"Forget it. Tell me what you see," I said, to get his mind back where I wanted it.

"The diamonds . . ." he said.

He launched into a long, disjointed monologue. I listened. Every now and then I said something to return him to the theme of the diamonds, and I kept throwing out Rudy Myers' name. His responses remained fragmentary, but the picture did begin to emerge.

I hurried then, trying to learn as much as I could before Barthelme returned and decompressed us any further. I was afraid that it would sober him up suddenly, because decompression works that way when you hit the right point in nitrogen-narcosis cases. He and Mike seemed to have been bringing in the diamonds, all right —from where, I did not learn. Whenever I tried to find out whether Frank had been disposing of them for them, he began muttering endearments to Linda. The part I hammered away most at began to come clear, however.

Mike must have said something one time, in the ashram back of the Chickcharny. It must have interested Rudy sufficiently so that he put together a specialty of the house other than a Pink Paradise for him—apparently, several times. These could have been the bad trips I had heard about. Whatever Rudy served him, he got the story out of him and saw dollar signs. Only Paul proved a lot tougher than he had thought. When he made his request for hush money and Mike told Paul about it, Paul came up with the idea for the mad dolphin in the park and got Mike to go along with it, persuading Rudy to meet him there for a payoff. Then things got sort of hazy, because the mention of dolphins kept setting him off. But he had apparently waited at a prearranged point, and the two of them took care of Rudy when that point was reached, one holding him, the other working him over with the jawbone. It was not clear whether Mike was injured fighting with Rudy and Paul then decided to finish him off and make him look like a dolphin slashee also, or whether he had planned that part carefully too and simply turned on Mike afterward, taking him by surprise. Either way, their friendship had been declining steadily for some time and the blackmail business had driven the final nail into the lid.

That was the story I got, punctuated rather than phrased by his responses to my oblique questioning. Apparently, killing Mike had bothered him more than he had thought it would, also. He kept calling me Mike, kept saying he was sorry, and I kept redirecting his attention.

Before I could get any more out of him, Barthelme came back and asked me how he was doing.

"Babbling," I replied. "That's all."

"I'm going to decompress some more. That might straighten him out. We're on our way now, and there will be someone waiting."

"Good."

But it did not straighten him out. He remained exactly the same. I tried to take advantage, to get more out of him—specifically, the source of the diamonds—but something went wrong. His nirvana switched over to some version of hell.

He launched himself at my throat, and I had to fight him off, push him back, hold him in place. He sagged then, commenced weeping, and began muttering of the horrors he was witnessing. I talked slowly, softly, soothingly, trying to guide him back to the earlier, happier part of things. But nothing worked, so I shut up, stayed silent and kept my guard up.

He drowsed then, and Barthelme continued to decompress us. I kept an eye on Paul's breathing and checked his pulse periodically, but nothing seemed amiss in that area.

We were fully decompressed by the time we docked, and I undogged the hatch and chucked out our gear. Paul stirred at that, opened his eyes, stared at me, then said, "That was weird."

"How do you feel now?"

"All right, I think. But very tired and kind of shaky."

"Let me give you a hand."

"Thanks."

I helped him out and assisted him down the plank to a waiting wheelchair. A young doctor was there, as were the Cashels, Deems, and Carter. I could not help wondering what was going on at the moment inside Paul's head. The doctor checked his heartbeat, pulse, blood pressure, shined a light into his eyes and ears, and had him touch the tip of his nose a couple of times. Then he nodded and gestured, and Barthelme began wheeling him toward the dispensary. The doctor walked along part of the way, talking with them. Then he returned while they went on, and he asked me to tell him everything that had happened.

So I did, omitting only the substance I had derived from the babbling part. Then he thanked me and turned toward the dispensary once more.

I caught up with him quickly.

"What does it look like?" I asked.

"Nitrogen narcosis," he replied.

"Didn't it take a rather peculiar form?" I said. "I mean, the way he responded to decompression and all?"

He shrugged.

"People come in all shapes and sizes, inside as well as out," he said. "Do a complete physical on a man and you still can't tell what he'd be like if he got drunk, say —loud, sad, belligerent, sleepy. The same with this. He seems to be out of it now, though."

"No complications?"

"Well, I'm going to do an EKG as soon as we get him to the dispensary. But I think he's all right. —Listen, is there a decompression chamber in the dispensary?"

"Most likely. But I'm new here. I'm not certain."

"Well, why don't you come along until we find out? If there isn't one, I'd like to have that submersible unit moved over."

"Oh?"

"Just a precaution. I want him to stay in the dispensary overnight, with someone around to keep an eye on him. If there should be a recurrence, I want the machine handy so he can be recompressed right away."

"I see."

We caught up with Barthelme at the door. The others were there also.

"Yes, there is a unit inside," Barthelme told him, "and I'll sit up with him."

Everyone volunteered. though, and the night was finally divided into three shifts—Barthelme, Frank, and Andy, respectively. Each of them, of course, was quite familiar with decompression equipment.

Frank came up and touched my arm.

"Nothing much we can really do here now," he said. "Shall we go have that dinner?"

"Oh?" I said, automatically glancing at my watch.

"So we eat at seven instead of six thirty," he said, chuckling.

"Fine. That will give me time to shower and change."

"Okay. Come right over as soon as you're ready. We'll still have time for a drink."

"All right. I'm thirsty. —See you soon."

I went on back to my place and got cleaned up. No new billets-doux, and the stones were still in the disposal unit. I combed my hair and started back across the islet.

As I neared the dispensary. the doctor emerged, talking back over his shoulder to someone in the doorway. Barthelme, probably. As I approached, I saw that he was carrying his bag.

He withdrew, began to move away. He nodded and smiled when he saw me.

"I think your friend will be all right," he said.

"Good. That is just what I was going to ask you."

"How do *you* feel?"

"All right. Fine, actually."

"You have had no symptoms at all. Correct?"

"That's right."

"Fine. If you were to, you know where to go. Right?"

"Indeed."

"Okay, then. I'll be geing now."

"So long."

He headed off toward a tiny hopper he had landed near the main lab. I continued on over to Frank's place.

Frank came out to meet me.

"What did the doctor have to say?" he asked.

"That everything looks all right," I told him.

"Uh-huh. Come on in and tell me what you're drinking."

He opened the door, held it.

"A bourbon would be nice," I said.

"With anything?"

"Just ice."

"Okay. Linda's out back, setting things on the table."

He moved about, putting together a pair of drinks. I wondered whether he was going to say anything about the diamond business now, while we were alone. But he didn't.

He turned, passed me my drink, raised his in a brief salute, took a sip.

"Tell me all about it," he said.

"All right."

The telling lasted into dinner and out of it again. I was very hungry, Linda was quite quiet, and Frank kept asking questions, drawing out every detail of Paul's discomfort, distress. I wondered about Linda and Frank. I could not see her keeping her affair secret on a small place like the station. What did Frank really know, think, feel about it? What was the true function of their triangle in this bizarre case?

I sat with them for a while after dinner, and I could almost feel the tension between the two of them, a thing he seemed set on dealing with by keeping the conversation moving steadily along the lines he had established, she by withdrawing from it. I had no doubt that it had been precipitated by Paul's mishap, but I came to feel more and more awkward in my role as a buffer against an approaching quarrel, a confrontation, or the renewal of an old one. Thanking them for the meal, I excused myself as soon as I could, pleading a weariness that was half real.

Frank got to his feet immediately.

"I'll walk you back," he said.

"All right."

So he did.

As we neared my place, he finally said it.

"About those stones . . ."

"Yes?"

"You're sure there are lots more where they came from?"

"Come this way," I said, leading him around the cottage to the patio and turning when we reached it. "Just in time for the last couple of minutes of sunset. Beautiful. Why don't you watch it finish up? I'll be right back."

I let myself in through the rear door, moved to the sink, and got the disposal unit open. It took me a minute or so to work the bag out. I opened it, seized a double fistful, and carried them back outside.

"Cup your hands," I said to him.

He did, and I filled them.

"How's that?"

He raised them, moved nearer the light spilling through the open door.

"My God!" he said. "You really do!"

"Of course."

"All right. I'll dispose of them for you. Thirty-five percent."

"Twenty-five is tops. Like I said."

"I know of a gem-and-mineral show a week from Saturday. A man I know could be there if I gave him a call. He'd pay a good price. I'll call him—for thirty percent."

"Twenty-five."

"It's a pity we are so close and can't quite come to terms. We both lose that way."

"Oh, all right. Thirty it is."

I took back the stones and dumped them into my pockets, and we shook on it. Then Frank turned.

"I'm going over to the lab now," he said. "See what's the matter with that unit you brought back."

"Let me know when you find out, will you? I'd like to know."

"Sure."

He went away and I restashed the gems, fetched a dolphin book, and began to page through it. Then it struck me just how funny it was, the way things were working out. All the talk about dolphins, all my reading, speculating, including a long philosophical dissertation on their hypothetical dreamsongs as a religio-diagogical form of *ludus*—for what? To find that it was probably all unnecessary? To realize that I would probably get through the entire case without even seeing a dolphin?

Well, that was what I had wanted, of course, what Don and Lydia Barnes and the Institute wanted—for me to clear the good name of the dolphin. Still, what a tangled mess it was turning out to be! Blackmail, murder, diamond smuggling, with a little adultery tossed in on the side. . . . How was I going to untangle it sweetly and neatly, clear the suspects—who were out practicing their *ludus* and not giving a damn about the whole business —and then fade from the picture, as is my wont, without raising embarrassing questions, without seeming to have been especially involved?

A feeling of profound jealousy of the dolphin came over me and did not entirely vanish. Did they ever create problem situations of this order among themselves? I strongly doubted it. Maybe if I collected enough green karma stamps I could put in for dolphin next time around. . . .

Everything caught up with me, and I dozed off with the light still burning.

A sharp, insistent drumming awakened me.

I rubbed my eyes, stretched. The noise came again, and I turned in that direction.

It was the window. Someone was rapping on the frame. I rose and crossed over, saw that it was Frank.

"Yeah?" I said. "What's up?"

"Come on out," he said. "It's important."

"Okay. Just a minute."

I went and rinsed my face, to complete the waking-up process and give me a chance to think. A glance at my watch showed me that it was around ten-thirty.

When I finally stepped outside, he seized my shoulder.

"Come on! Damn it! I told you it was important!"

I fell into step with him.

"All right! I had to wake up. What's the matter?"

"Paul's dead," he said.

"What?"

"You heard me. Dead."

"How'd it happen?"

"He stopped breathing."

"They usually do. —But how did it happen?"

"I'd gotten to fooling with the unit you'd brought back. It's over there now. I moved it in when my time came to relieve Barthelme, so that I could keep working on it. Anyway, I got so involved that I wasn't paying much attention to him. When I finally did check on him again, he was dead. That's all. His face was dark and twisted. Some sort of lung failure, it seems. Maybe there was an air embolism. . . ."

We entered the rear of the building, the nearest entrance, the water splashing softly behind us, a light breeze following us in. We passed the recently set-up workbench, tools and the partly dismantled sonic unit spread across its surface. Rounding the corner to our left, we entered the room where Paul lay. I switched the light on.

His face was no longer handsome, bearing now the signs of one who had spent his final moments fighting for breath. I crossed to him, felt for a pulse, knew in advance I would find none. I covered a fingernail with my thumb and squeezed. It remained white when I released it.

"How long ago?" I asked.

"Right before I came for you."

"Why me?"

"You were nearest."

"I see.—Was the sheet torn in this place before, I wonder?"

"I don't know."

"There were no cries, no sounds at all?"

"I didn't hear anything. If I had, I would have come right away."

I felt a sudden desire for a cigarette, but there were oxygen tanks in the room and NO SMOKING signs all over the building. I turned and retraced my steps, pushed the door open, held it with my back—leaning against it —lit a cigarette, and stared out across the water.

"Very neat," I said then. "With the day's symptoms behind him, he'll warrant a 'natural causes' with a 'possible air embolism,' 'congestive lung failure,' or some damn thing behind it."

"What do you mean?" Frank demanded.

"Was he sedated? —I don't know. It doesn't matter. I'd imagine you used the recompressor. Right? Or did you tough it out and just smother him?"

"Come off it. Why would I—"

"In a way, I helped kill him," I said. "I thought he was safe with you here because you hadn't done anything about him all this time. You wanted to keep her, to win her back. Spending a lot of money on her was one way you tried. But it was a vicious circle, because Paul was a part of your source of extra revenue. Then I came along and offered an alternative supply. Then today's accident, the whole setup here tonight . . . You rose to the occasion, seized the opportunity, and slammed the barn door. Not to mention striking while the iron was hot. —Congratulations. I think you'll get away with it. Because this is all guesswork, of course. There is no real proof. Good show."

He sighed.

"Then why go into all that? It's over. We will go see Barthelme now and you will talk because I will be too distraught."

"But I'm curious about Rudy and Mike. I've been wondering all along. Did you have any part in it when they got theirs?"

"What do you know?" he asked slowly. "And how do you know it?"

"I know that Paul and Mike were the source of the stones. I know that Rudy found out and tried to blackmail them. They dealt with him, and I think Paul took care of Mike for good measure at the same time. How do I know? Paul babbled all the way back this afternoon and I was in the decompressor with him, remember? I learned about the diamonds, the murders, and about Linda and Paul, just by listening."

He leaned back against the workbench. He shook his head.

"I was suspicious of you," he said, "but you had the diamonds for proof. You came across them awfully fast, I'll admit. But I accepted your story because of the possibility that Paul's deposit was really somewhere quite near. He never told me where it was, either. I decided you had to have either stumbled across it or followed him to it and known enough to recognize it for what it was. Whichever way, though, it doesn't matter. I would rather do business with you. Shall we just leave the whole thing at that?"

"If you will tell me about Rudy and Mike."

"I don't really know any more than what you've just said. That was none of my affair. Paul took care of everything. Answer one for me now: How did you find the deposit?"

"I didn't," I said. "I haven't the least idea where he got them."

He straightened.

"I don't believe you! The stones—where did they come from?"

"I found where Paul had hidden a bag of them. I stole it."

"Why?"

"Money, of course."

"Then why did you lie to me about where you got them?"

"You think I'd come out and say they were stolen? Now, though——"

He came forward very fast, and I saw that he had a large wrench in his hand.

I jumped backward, and the door caught him on the shoulder as it snapped inward. It only slowed him for an instant, though. He burst through and was at me again. I continued my retreat, falling into a defensive position.

He swung and I dodged to the side, chopping at his elbow. We both missed. His backstroke grazed my shoulder then, so that the blow I did land, seconds later, fell near his kidney with less force than I had hoped for. I danced back as he swung again, and my kick caught him on the hip. He dropped to one knee, but was up again before I could press in, swinging toward my head. I backed farther and he stalked me.

I could hear the water, smell it. I wondered about diving in. He was awfully close. . . .

When he came in again, I twisted back and grabbed for his arm. I caught hold near the elbow and hung on, hooking my fingers toward his face. He drove himself into me then and I fell, still clutching his arm, catching hold of his belt with my other hand. My shoulder smashed against the ground, and he was on top of me, wrestling to free his arm. As he succeeded in dragging it away, his weight came off me for an instant. Pulling free, I doubled myself into a ball and kicked out with both legs.

They connected. I heard him grunt.

Then he was gone.

I heard him splashing about in the water. I also heard distant voices, calling, approaching us from across the islet.

I regained my feet. I moved toward the edge.

Then he screamed—a long, awful, agonized wail. By the time I reached the edge, it had ceased.

When Barthelme came up beside me, he stopped repeating "What happened?" as soon as he looked down and saw the flashing fins at the center of the turmoil. Then he said, "Oh, my God!" And then nothing.

In my statement, later, I said that he had seemed highly agitated when he had come to get me, that he told me Paul had stopped breathing, that I had returned with him to the dispensary, determined that Paul was indeed dead, said so, and asked him for the details; that as we were talking he seemed to get the impression that I thought he had been negligent and somehow contributed to the death; that he had grown further agitated and finally attacked me; that we had fought and he had fallen into the water. All of which, of course, was correct. Deponent sinneth only by omission. They seemd to buy it. They went away. The shark hung around, waiting for dessert perhaps, and the dolphin people came and anesthetized him and took him away. Barthelme told me the damaged sonic projector could indeed have been shorting intermittently.

So Paul had killed Rudy and Mike; Frank had killed Paul and then been killed himself by the shark on whom the first two killings could now be blamed. The dolphins were cleared, and there was no one left to bring to justice for anything. The source of the diamonds was now one of life's numerous little mysteries.

. . . So, after everyone had departed, the statements

been taken, the remains of the remains removed—long after that, as the night hung late, clear, clean, with its bright multitudes doubled in their pulsing within the cool flow of the Gulf Stream about the station, I sat in a deck chair on the small patio behind my quarters, drinking a can of beer and watching the stars go by.

. . . I needed but stamp CLOSED on my mental file.

But who had written me the note, the note that had set the infernal machine to chugging?

Did it really matter, now that the job was done? As long as they kept quiet about me. . . .

I took another sip of beer.

Yes, it did, I decided. I might as well look around a bit more.

I withdrew a cigarette and moved to light it . . .

When I pulled into the harbor, the lights were on. As I climbed to the pier, her voice came to me over a loud-speaker.

She greeted me by name—my real name, which I hadn't heard spoken in a long while—and she asked me to come in.

I moved across the pier and up to the front of the building. The door stood ajar. I entered.

It was a long, low room, completely Oriental in decor. she wore a green silk kimono. She knelt on the floor, a tea service laid before her.

"Please come and be seated," she said.

I nodded, removed my shoes, crossed the room, and sat down.

"*O-cha do desu-ka?*" she asked.

"*Itadakimasu.*"

She poured, and we sipped tea for a time. After the second cup I drew an ashtray toward me.

"Cigarette?" I asked.

"I don't smoke," she said. "But I wish you would. I try to take as few noxious substances into my own system as possible. I suppose that is how the whole thing began."

I lit one for me.

"I've never met a genuine telepath before," I said, "that I know of."

"I'd trade it for a sound body," she said, "any day. It wouldn't even have to be especially attractive."

"I don't suppose there is even a real need for me to ask my questions," I said.

"No," she said, "not really. How free do you think our wills might be?"

"Less every day," I said.

She smiled.

"I asked that," she said, "because I have thought a lot about it of late. I thought of a little girl I once knew, a girl who lived in a garden of terrible flowers. They were beautiful, and they were there to make her happy to look upon. But they could not hide their odor from her, and that was the odor of pity. For she was a sick little girl. So it was not their colors and textures from which she fled, but rather the fragrance which few knew she could detect. It was a painful thing to smell it constantly, and so in solitude she found her something of peace. Had it not been for her ability she would have remained in the garden."

She paused to take a sip of tea.

"One day she found friends," she continued, "in an unexpected place. The dolphin is a joyous fellow, his heart uncluttered with the pity that demeans. The way of knowing that had set her apart, had sent her away, here brought her close. She came to know the hearts, the thoughts of her new friends more perfectly than men know those of one another. She came to love them, to be one of their family."

She took another sip of tea, then sat in silence for a time, staring into the cup.

"There are great ones among them," she said finally, "such as you guessed at earlier. Prophet, seer, philoso-

pher, musician—there is no man-made word I know of
to describe this sort of one, or the function he performs.
There are, however, those among them who voice the
dreamsong with particular subtlety and profundity—
something like music, yet not, drawn from that timeless
place in themselves where perhaps they look upon the
infinite, then phrase it for their fellows. The greatest I
have ever known"—and she clicked the syllables in a
high-pitched tone—"bears something like 'Kjwalll'kje'k-
'koothaïlll'kje'k for name or title. I could no more explain his dreamsong to you than I could explain Mozart
to one who had never heard music. But when he, in his
place, came to be threatened, I did what must be done."

"You see that I fail to see," I said, lowering my cup.

She refilled it, and then, "The Chickcharny is built up
over the water," she said, and a vision of it came clear,
disturbingly real, into my mind. "Like that," she said.

"I do not drink strong beverages, I do not smoke, I
seldom take medication," she said. "This is not a matter
of choice. It is a physiological rule I break at my own
peril. But should I not enjoy the same things others of
my kind may know, just as I now enjoy the cigarette we
are smoking?"

"I begin to see—"

"Swimming beneath the ashram at night, I could ride
the mounting drug dreams of that place, know the
peace, the happiness, the joy, and withdraw if it turned
to something else—"

"Mike—" I said.

"Yes, it was he who led me to 'Kjwalll'kje'k-
'koothaïlll'kje'k, all unknowing. I saw there the place
where they had found the diamonds. I see that you think
it is near Martinique, since I was there just recently. I
will not answer you on this. I saw there too, however,
the idea of hurting dolphins. It seemed that they had
been driven away from the place of their discovery—
though not harmed—by dolphins. Several times. I found
this so unusual that I was moved to investigate, and I

learned that it was true. The place of their discovery was in the area of his song. He dwells in those waters, and others come to hear him there. It is, in this sense, a special place, because of his presence. They were seeking a way to ensure their own safety when they returned for more of the stones," she went on. "They learned of the effects of the noises of the killer whale for this purpose. But they also obtained explosives, should the recording prove insufficient over a period of days.

"The two killings occurred while I was away," she said. "You are essentially correct as to what was done. I had not known they would take place, nor would my telling of Paul's thoughts ever be admissible in any court. He used everything he every got his hands or mind around, that man—however poor his grasp. He took Frank's theory as well as his wife, learned just enough to find the stones, with a little luck. Luck—he had that for a long while. He learned just enough about dolphins to know of the effects of the sounds of the killer whale, but not how they would behave if they had to fight, to kill. And even there he was lucky. The story was accepted. Not by everybody. But it was given sufficient credence. He was safe, and he planned to go back to—the place. I sought a way to stop him. And I wanted to see the dolphins vindicated—but that was of secondary importance then. Then you appeared, and I knew that I had found it. I went to the station at night, crawled ashore, left you a note."

"And you damaged the sonic-broadcast unit?"

"Yes."

"You did it at such a time that you knew Paul and I would go down together to replace it."

"Yes."

"And the other?"

"Yes, that too. I filled Paul's mind with things I had felt and seen beneath the ashram of the Chickcharny."

"And you could look into Frank's mind as well. You knew how he would react. You set up the murder!"

"I did not force him to do anything. Is not his will as free as our own?"

I looked down into the tea, troubled by the thought. I gulped it. Then I stared at her.

"Did you not control him, even a little, near the end, when he attacked me? Or—far more important—what of a more rudimentary nervous system? Could you control the actions of a shark?"

She refilled my teacup.

"Of course not," she said.

We sat for another silent time. Then, "What did you try to do to me when I decided to continue my investigation?" I asked. "Were you not trying to baffle my senses and drive me to destruction?"

"No," she said quickly. "I was watching you to see what you would decide. You frightened me with your decision. But what I did was not an attack, at first. I tried to show you something of the dreamsong, to sooth you, to put you at peace. I had hoped that such an experience might work some mental alchemy, would soften your resolve—"

"You would have accompanied it with suggestions to that effect."

"Yes, I would have. But then you burned yourself and the pain pulled you back. That was when I attacked you."

She suddenly sounded tired. But then, it had been a very busy day for her, all things considered.

"And this was my mistake," she said. "Had I simply let you go on, you would have had nothing. But you saw the unnatural nature of the attack. You associated it with Paul's raptures, and you thought of me—a mutant—and of dolphins and diamonds and my recent trip. It all spilled into your mind—and then the threat that I saw you could keep: alluvial diamonds and Martinique, into the Central Data Bank. I had to call you then, to talk."

"What now?" I asked. "No court could ever convict

you of anything. You are safe. *I* can hardly condemn you. My own hands are not free of blood, as you must know. You are the only person alive who knows who I am, and that makes me uncomfortable. Yet I have some guesses concerning things you would not like known. You will not try to destroy me, for you know what I will do with these guesses if you fail."

"And I see that you will not use your ring unless you are provoked. Thank you. I have feared it."

"It appears that we have reached something of a standoff."

"Then why do we not both forget?"

"You mean—trust each other?"

"Is it so novel a thing?"

"You must admit you are possessed of a small edge in such matters."

"True. But it is of value only for the moment. People change. It does not show me what you will be thinking on another day, in some other place. You are in a better position to know that, for you have known yourself far longer than I."

"True, I suppose."

"I, of course, really have nothing to gain by destroying the pattern of your existence. You, on the other hand, could conceivably be moved to seek an unrecorded source of income."

"I can't deny that," I said. "But if I gave you my word, I would keep it."

"I know that you mean that. I also know that you believe much of what I have said, with some reservations."

I nodded.

"You do not really understand the significance of 'Kjwalll'kje'k'koothaïlll'kje'k.'"

"How could I, not being a dolphin or even a telepath?"

"May I show you what it is that I am seeking to preserve, to defend?"

I thought about it for a time, recalling those recent

moments back at the station when she had hit me with something out of William James. I had no way of knowing what manner of control, what sort of powers she might be able to exercise upon me if I agreed to some experiment along these lines. However, if things got out of control, if there was the least feeling of meddling with my mind, beyond the thing itself, I knew a way to terminate the experience instantly. I folded my hands before me, laying two fingers upon my ring.

"Very well," I said.

And then it began again, something like music, yet not, some development of a proposition that could not be verbalized, for its substance was of a stuff that no man possessed or perceived, lying outside the range of human sensory equipment. I realized then that that part of me which experienced this had its place temporarily in the mind of the statement's creator, that this was the dreamsong of 'Kjwalll'kje'k'koothaïlll'kje'k, that I witnessed/participated in the timeless argument as he improvised, orchestrated it, drawing entire sections of previously constructed visions and phrasings, perfect and pure, from a memory so vital that its workings were barely distinguishable from the activities of the moment, and blending these into fresh harmonies to a joyous rhythm I comprehended only obliquely, through the simultaneous sensing of his own pleasure in the act of their formulation.

I felt the delight in this dance of thought, rational though not logical; the process, like all of art, was an answer to something, though precisely what, I did not know nor really care; for it was, in and of itself, a sufficiency of being—and if one day it were to provide me with an emotional weapon at a time when I would otherwise stand naked and alone, why this was one of the things none has the right to expect, yet sometimes discovers within the recollection of such fragments of existence cast by a special seer with a kind of furious joy.

I forgot my own being, abandoned my limited range

of senses as I swam in a sea that was neither dark nor light, formed nor formless, yet knowing my way, subsumed, as it were, within a perpetual act of that thing we had decided to call *ludus* that was creation, destruction, and sustenance, patterned and infinitely repatterned, scattered and joined, mounting and descending, divorced from all temporal phenomena yet containing the essence of time. Time's soul it seemed I was, the infinite potentialities that fill the moment, surrounding and infusing the tiny stream of existence, and joyous, joyous, joyous . . .

Spinning, my mind came away, and I sat, still clutching my death ring, across from the little girl who had fled from the terrible flowers, now clad in wet green and very, very wan.

"O-cha do desu-ka?" she asked.

"Itadakimasu."

She poured. I wanted to reach out and touch her hand, but I raised the teacup instead and sipped from it.

She had my answer, of course. She knew.

But she spoke, after a time: "When my moment comes—who knows how soon?—I shall go to him," she said. "I shall be there, with 'Kjwalll'kje'k'koothaïlll'kje'k. Who knows but that I shall continue, as a memory perhaps, in that timeless place, as a part of the dreamsong? But then, I feel a part of it now."

"I—"

She raised her hand. We finished our tea in silence.

I did not really want to go then, but I knew that I must.

There were so many things that I might have said, I thought, as I headed the *Isabella* back toward Station One, my bag of diamonds, and all the other things and people I had left behind, waiting for me to touch them or speak to them.

But then, I reflected, the best words are often those left unsaid.

PART THREE

Home Is the Hangman

Big fat flakes down the night, silent night, windless night. And I never count them as storms unless there is wind. Not a sigh or whimper, though. Just a cold, steady whiteness, drifting down outside the window, and a silence confirmed by gunfire, driven deeper now that it had ceased. In the main room of the lodge the only sounds were the occasional hiss and sputter of the logs turning to ashes on the grate.

I sat in a chair turned sidewise from the table to face the door. A tool kit rested on the floor to my left. The helmet stood on the table, a lopsided basket of metal, quartz, porcelain, and glass. If I heard the click of a microswitch followed by a humming sound from within it, then a faint light would come on beneath the meshing near to its forward edge and begin to blink rapidly. If these things occurred, there was a very strong possibility that I was going to die.

I had removed a black ball from my pocket when Larry and Bert had gone outside, armed, respectively, with a flame thrower and what looked like an elephant gun. Bert had also taken two grenades with him.

I unrolled the black ball, opening it out into a seamless glove, a dollop of something resembling moist putty stuck to its palm. Then I drew the glove on over my left hand and sat with it upraised, elbow resting on the arm of the chair. A small laser flash pistol in which I had very little faith lay beside my right hand on the tabletop, next to the helmet.

If I were to slap a metal surface with my left hand, the substance would adhere there, coming free of the glove. Two seconds later it would explode, and the force of the explosion would be directed in against the surface. Newton would claim his own by way of right-angled redistributions of the reaction, hopefully tearing lateral hell out of the contact surface. A smother-charge, it was called, and its possession came under concealed-weapons and possession-of-burglary-tools statutes in most places. The molecularly gimmicked goo, I decided, was great stuff. It was just the delivery system that left more to be desired.

Beside the helmet, next to the gun, in front of my hand, stood a small walkie-talkie. This was for purposes of warning Bert and Larry if I should hear the click of a microswitch followed by a humming sound, should see a light come on and begin to blink rapidly. Then they would know that Tom and Clay, with whom we had lost contact when the shooting began, had failed to destroy the enemy and doubtless lay lifeless at their stations now, a little over a kilometer to the south. Then they would know that they, too, were probably about to die.

I called out to them when I heard the click. I picked up the helmet and rose to my feet as its light began to blink.

But it was already too late.

The fourth place listed on the Christmas card I had sent Don Walsh the previous year was Peabody's Book Shop and Beer Stube in Baltimore, Maryland. Accordingly, on the last night in October I sat in its rearmost room, at the final table before the alcove with the door leading to the alley. Across that dim chamber, a woman dressed in black played the ancient upright piano, uptempoing everything she touched. Off to my right, a fire wheezed and spewed fumes on a narrow hearth beneath a crowded mantelpiece overseen by an ancient and antlered profile. I sipped a beer and listened to the sounds.

I half hoped that this would be one of the occasions when Don failed to show up. I had sufficient funds to hold me through spring and I did not really feel like working. I had summered farther north, was anchored now in the Chesapeake, and was anxious to continue Caribbeanward. A growing chill and some nasty winds told me I had tarried overlong in these latitudes. Still, the understanding was that I remain in the chosen bar until midnight. Two hours to go.

I ate a sandwich and ordered another beer. About halfway into it, I spotted Don approaching the entrance-way, topcoat over his arm, head turning. I manufactured a matching quantity of surprise when he appeared beside my table with a, "Ron! Is that really you?"

I rose and clasped his hand.

"Alan! Small world, or something like that. Sit down! Sit down!"

He settled onto the chair across from me, draped his coat over the one to his left.

"What are you doing in this town?" he asked.

"Just a visit," I answered. "Said hello to a few friends." I patted the scars, the stains on the venerable surface before me. "And this is my last stop. I'll be leaving in a few hours."

He chuckled.

"Why is it that you knock on wood?"

I grinned.

"I was expressing affection for one of Henry Mencken's favorite speakeasies."

"This place dates back that far?"

I nodded.

"It figures," he said. "You've got this thing for the past—or against the present. I'm never sure which."

"Maybe a little of both," I said. "I wish Mencken would stop in. I'd like his opinion on the present. — What are you doing with it?"

"What?"

"The present. Here. Now."

"Oh." He spotted the waitress and ordered a beer. "Business trip," he said then. "To hire a consultant."

"Oh. How *is* business?"

"Complicated," he said, "complicated."

We lit cigarettes and after a while his beer arrived. We smoked and drank and listened to the music.

I've sung this song and I'll sing it again: the world is like an uptempoed piece of music. Of the many changes which came to pass during my lifetime, it seems that the majority have occurred during the past few years. It also struck me that way several years ago, and I'd a hunch I might be feeling the same way a few years hence—that is, if Don's business did not complicate me off this mortal coil or condenser before then.

Don operates the second-largest detective agency in the world, and he sometimes finds me useful because I do not exist. I do not exist now because I existed once at the time and the place where we attempted to begin scoring the wild ditty of our times. I refer to the world Central Data Bank project and the fact that I had had a significant part in that effort to construct a working model of the real world, accounting for everyone and everything in it. How well we succeeded, and whether possession of the world's likeness does indeed provide its custodians with a greater measure of control over its functions, are questions my former colleagues still debate as the music grows more shrill and you can't see the maps for the pins. I made my decision back then and saw to it that I did not receive citizenship in that second world, a place which may now have become more important than the first. Exiled to reality, my own sojourns across the line are necessarily those of an alien guilty of illegal entry. I visit periodically because I go where I must to make my living. —That is where Don comes in. The people I can become are often very useful when he has peculiar problems.

Unfortunately, at that moment, it seemed that he did,

just when the whole gang of me felt like turning down the volume and loafing.

We finished our drinks, got the bill, settled it.

"This way," I said, indicating the rear door, and he swung into his coat and followed me out.

"Talk here?" he asked, as we walked down the alley.

"Rather not," I said. "Public transportation, then private conversation."

He nodded and came along.

About three-quarters of an hour later we were in the saloon of the *Proteus* and I was making coffee. We were rocked gently by the Bay's chill waters, under a moonless sky. I'd only a pair of the smaller lights burning. Comfortable. On the water, aboard the *Proteus*, the crowding, the activities, the tempo, of life in the cities, on the land, are muted, slowed—fictionalized—by the metaphysical distancing a few meters of water can provide. We alter the landscape with great facility, but the ocean has always seemed unchanged, and I suppose by extension we are infected with some feelings of timelessness whenever we set out upon her. Maybe that's one of the reasons I spend so much time there.

"First time you've had me aboard," he said. "Comfortable. Very."

"Thanks. —Cream? Sugar?"

"Yes. Both."

We settled back with our steaming mugs and I asked, "What have you got?"

"One case involving two problems," he said. "One of them sort of falls within my area of competence. The other does not. I was told that it is an absolutely unique situation and would require the services of a very special specialist."

"I'm not a specialist at anything but keeping alive."

His eyes came up suddenly and caught my own.

"I had always assumed that you knew an awful lot about computers," he said.

I looked away. That was hitting below the belt. I had

never held myself out to him as an authority in that area, and there had always been a tacit understanding between us that my methods of manipulating circumstance and identity were not open to discussion. On the other hand, it was obvious to him that my knowledge of the system was both extensive and intensive. Still, I didn't like talking about it. So I moved to defend.

"Computer people are a dime a dozen," I said. "It was probably different in your time, but these days they start teaching computer science to little kids their first year in school. So sure, I know a lot about it. This generation, everybody does."

"You know that is not what I meant," he said. "Haven't you known me long enough to trust me a little more than that? The question springs solely from the case at hand. That's all."

I nodded. Reactions by their very nature are not always appropriate, and I had invested a lot of emotional capital in a heavy-duty set. So, "Okay, I know more about them than the school kids," I said.

"Thanks. That can be our point of departure." He took a sip of coffee. "My own background is in law and accounting, followed by the military, military intelligence, and civil service, in that order. Then I got into this business. What technical stuff I know I've picked up along the way—a scrap here, a crash course there. I know a lot about what things can *do*, not so much about how they *work*. I did not understand the details on this one, so I want you to start at the top and explain things to me, for as far as you can go. I need the background review, and if you are able to furnish it I will also know that you are the man for the job. You can begin by telling me how the early space-exploration robots worked —like, say the ones they used on Venus."

"That's not computers," I said, "and for that matter, they weren't really robots. They were telefactoring devices."

"Tell me what makes the difference."

"A robot is a machine which carries out certain operations in accordance with a program of instructions. A telefactor is a slave machine operated by remote control. The telefactor functions in a feedback situation with its operator. Depending on how sophisticated you want to get, the links can be audiovisual, kinesthetic, tactile, even olfactory. The more you want to go in this direction, the more anthropomorphic you get in the thing's design.

"In the case of Venus, if I recall correctly, the human operator in orbit wore an exoskeleton which controlled the movements of the body, legs, arms, and hands of the device on the surface below, receiving motion and force feedback through a system of airjet transducers. He had on a helmet controlling the slave device's television camera—set, obviously enough, in its turret—which filled his field of vision with the scene below. He also wore earphones connected with its audio pickup. I read the book he wrote later. He said that for long stretches of time he would forget the cabin, forget that he was at the boss end of a control loop, and actually feel as if he were stalking through that hellish landscape. I remember being very impressed by it, just being a kid, and I wanted a super-tiny one all my own, so that I could wade around in puddles picking fights with microorganisms."

"Why?"

"Because there weren't any dragons on Venus. Anyhow, that is a telefactoring device, a thing quite distinct from a robot."

"I'm still with you," he said, and "Now tell me the difference between the early telefactoring devices and the later ones."

I swallowed some coffee.

"It was a bit trickier with respect to the outer planets and their satellites," I said. "There, we did not have orbiting operators at first. Economics, and some unresolved technical problems. Mainly economics. At any rate, the devices were landed on the target worlds, but the operators stayed home. Because of this, there was of course a time lag in the transmissions along the control loop. It took a while to receive the on-site input, and then there was another time lapse before the response movements reached the telefactor. We attempted to compensate for this in two ways: the first was by the employment of a simple wait–move, wait–move sequence; the second was more sophisticated and is actually the point where computers come into the picture in terms of participating in the control loop. It involved the setting up of models of known environmental factors, which were then enriched during the initial wait–move sequences. On this basis, the computer was then used to anticipate short-range developments. Finally, it could take over the loop and run it by a combination of 'predictor controls' and wait–move reviews. It still had to holler for human help, though, when unexpected things came up. So, with the outer planets, it was neither totally automatic nor totally manual—nor totally satisfactory—at first."

"Okay," he said, lighting a cigarette. "And the next step?"

"The next wasn't really a technical step forward in telefactoring. It was an economic shift. The pursestrings were loosened and we could afford to send men out. We landed them where we could land them, and in many of the places where we could not, we sent down the telefactors and orbited the men again. Like in the old days. The time-lag problem was removed because the operator was on top of things once more. If anything, you can look at it as a reversion to earlier methods. It is what we still often do, though, and it works."

He shook his head

"You left something out between the computers and the bigger budget."

I shrugged.

"A number of things were tried during that period,

but none of them proved as effective as what we already had going in the human–computer partnership with the telefactors."

"There was one project," he said, "which attempted to get around the time-lag troubles by sending the computer along with the telefactor as part of the package. Only the computer wasn't exactly a computer and the telefactor wasn't exactly a telefactor. Do you know which one I am referring to?"

I lit a cigarette of my own while I thought about it, then, "I think you are talking about the Hangman," I said.

"That's right and this is where I get lost. Can you tell me how it works?"

"Ultimately, it was a failure," I told him.

"But it worked at first."

"Aparently. But only on the easy stuff, on Io. It conked out later and had to be written off as a failure, albeit a noble one. The venture was overly ambitious from the very beginning. What seems to have happened was that the people in charge had the opportunity to combine vanguard projects—stuff that was still under investigation and stuff that was extremely new. In theory, it all seemed to dovetail so beautifully that they yeilded to the temptation and incorporated too much. It started out well, but it fell apart later."

"But what all was involved in the thing?"

"Lord! What wasn't? The computer that wasn't exactly a computer . . . Okay, we'll start there. Last century, three engineers at the University of Wisconsin— Nordman, Parmentier, and Scott—developed a device known as a superconductive tunnel-junction neuristor. Two tiny strips of metal with a thin insulating layer between. Supercool it and it passed electrical impulses without resistance. Surround it with magnetized material and pack a mass of them together—billions—and what have you got?"

He shook his head.

"Well, for one thing you've got an impossible situation to schematize when considering all the paths and interconnections that may be formed. There is an obvious similarity to the structure of the brain. So, they theorized, you don't even attempt to hook up such a device. You pulse in data and let it establish its own preferential pathways, by means of the magnetic material's becoming increasingly magnetized each time the current passes through it, thus cutting the resistance. The material establishes its own routes in a fashion analogous to the functioning of the brain when it is learning something.

"In the case of the Hangman, they used a setup very similar to this and they were able to pack over ten billion neuristor-type cells into a very small area—around a cubic foot. They aimed for that magic figure because that is approximately the number of nerve cells in the human brain. That is what I meant when I said that it wasn't really a computer. They were actually working in the area of artificial intelligence, no matter what they called it."

"If the thing had its own brain—computer or quasi-human—then it was a robot rather than a telefactor, right?"

"Yes and no and maybe," I said. "It was operated as a telefactor device here on Earth—on the ocean floor, in the desert, in mountainous country—as part of its programming. I suppose you could also call that its apprenticeship—or kindergarten. Perhaps that is even more appropriate. It was being shown how to explore in difficult environments and to report back. Once it mastered this, then theoretically they could hang it out there in the sky without a control loop and let it report its own findings."

"At that point would it be considered a robot?"

"A robot is a machine which carries out certain operations in accordance with a program of instructions. The Hangman made its *own* decisions, you see. And I suspect that by trying to produce something that close to the human brain in structure and function, the seemingly inevitable randomness of its model got included in. It wasn't just a machine following a program. It was too complex. That was probably what broke it down."

Don chuckled.

"Inevitable free will?"

"No. As I said, they had thrown too many things into one bag. Everybody and his brother with a pet project that might be fitted in seemed a supersalesman that season. For example, the psychophysics boys had a gimmick they wanted to try on it, and it got used. Ostensibly, The Hangman was a communications device. Actually, they were concerned as to whether the thing was truly sentient."

"Was it?"

"Apparently so, in a limited fashion. What they had come up with, to be made part of the initial telefactor loop, was a device which set up a weak induction field in the brain of the operator. The machine received and amplified the patterns of electrical activity being conducted in the Hangman's— might as well call it 'brain' —then passed them through a complex modulator and pulsed them into the induction field in the operator's head. —I am out of my area now and into that of Weber and Fechner, but a neuron has a threshold at which it will fire, and below which it will not. There are some forty thousand neurons packed together in a square millimeter of the cerebral cortex, in such a fashion that each one has several hundred synaptic connections with others about it. At any given moment, some of them may be way below the firing threshold while others are in a condition Sir John Eccles once referred to as 'critically poised'—ready to fire. If just one is pushed over the threshold, it can affect the discharge of hundreds of thousands of others within twenty milliseconds. The pulsating field was to provide such a push in a sufficiently selective fashion to give the operator an idea as to what was going on in the Hangman's brain. And vice versa. The Hangman was to have its own built-in version of the same thing. It was also thought that this might serve to humanize it somewhat, so that it would better appreciate the significance of its work—to instill something like loyalty, you might say."

"Do you think this could have contributed to its later breakdown?"

"Possibly. How can you say in a one-of-a-kind situation like this? If you want a guess, I'd say, 'Yes.' But it's just a guess."

"Uh-huh," he said, "and what were its physical capabilities?"

"Anthropomorphic design," I said, "both because it was originally telefactored and because of the psychological reasoning I just mentioned. It could pilot its own small vessel. No need for a life-support system, of course. Both it and the vessel were powered by fusion units, so that fuel was no real problem. Self-repairing. Capable of performing a great variety of sophisticated tests and measurements, of making observations, completing reports, learning new material, broadcasting its findings back here. Capable of surviving just about anywhere. In fact, it required less energy on the outer planets—less work for the refrigeration units, to maintain that supercooled brain in its midsection."

"How strong was it?"

"I don't recall all the specs. Maybe a dozen times as strong as a man, in things like lifting and pushing."

"It explored Io for us and started in on Europa."

"Yes."

"Then it began behaving erratically, just when we thought it had really learned its job."

"That sounds right," I said.

"It refused a direct order to explore Callisto, then headed out toward Uranus."

"Yes. It's been years since I read the reports. . . ."

"The malfunction worsened after that. Long periods

of silence interspersed with garbled transmissions. Now that I know more about its makeup, it almost sounds like a man going off the deep end."

"It seems similar."

"But it managed to pull itself together again for a brief while. It landed on Titania, began sending back what seemed like appropriate observation reports. This only lasted a short time, though. It went irrational once more, indicated that it was heading for a landing on Uranus itself, and that was it. We didn't hear from it after that. Now that I know about that mind-reading gadget I understand why a psychiatrist on this end could be so positive it would never function again."

"I never heard about that part."

"I did."

I shrugged. "This was all around twenty years ago," I said, "and, as I mentioned, it has been a long while since I've read anything about it."

"The Hangman's ship crashed or landed, as the case may be, in the Gulf of Mexico, two days ago."

I just stared at him.

"It was empty," Don went on, "when they finally got out and down to it."

"I don't understand."

"Yesterday morning," he continued, "restaurateur Manny Burns was found beaten to death in the office of his establishment, the Maison Saint-Michel, in New Orleans."

"I still fail to see—"

"Manny Burns was one of the four original operators who programmed—pardon me, 'taught'—the Hangman."

The silence lengthened, dragged its belly on the deck.

"Concidence . . . ?" I finally said.

"My client doesn't think so."

"Who is your client?"

"One of the three remaining members of the training group. He is convinced that the Hangman has returned to Earth to kill its former operators."

"Has he made his fears known to his old employers?"

"No."

"Why not?"

"Because it would require telling them the reason for his fears."

"That being . . . ?"

"He wouldn't tell me, either."

"How does he expect you to do a proper job?"

"He told me what he considered a proper job. He wanted two things done, neither of which requires a full case history. He wanted to be furnished with good bodyguards, and he wanted the Hangman found and disposed of. I have already taken care of the first part."

"And you want me to do the second?"

"That's right. You have confirmed my opinion that you are the man for the job."

"I see. Do you realize that if the thing is truly sentient this will be something very like murder? If it is not, of course, then it will only amount to the destruction of expensive government property."

"Which way do you look at it?"

"I look at it as a job," I said.

"You'll take it?"

"I need more facts before I can decide. Like, who is your client? Who are the other operators? Where do they live? What do they do? What—"

He raised his hand.

"First," he said, "the Honorable Jesse Brockden, senior Senator from Wisconsin, is our client. Confidentiality, of course, is written all over it."

I nodded. "I remember his being involved with the space program before he went into politics. I wasn't aware of the specifics, though. He could get government protection so easily—"

"To obtain it, he would apparently have to tell them something he doesn't want to talk about. Perhaps it

would hurt his career. I simply do not know. He doesn't
want them. He wants us."

I nodded again.

"What about the others? Do they want us, too?"

"Quite the opposite. They don't subscribe to Brockden's notions at all. They seem to think he is something
of a paranoid."

"How well do they know one another these days?"

"They live in different parts of the country, haven't
seen each other in years. Been in occasional touch,
though."

"Kind of a flimsy basis for that diagnosis, then."

"One of them *is* a psychiatrist."

"Oh. Which one?"

"Leila Thackery is her name. Lives in St. Louis.
Works at the State Hospital there."

"None of them have gone to any authority, then—
federal or local?"

"That's right. Brockden contacted them when he
heard about the Hangman. He was in Washington at the
time. Got word on its return right away and managed to
get the story killed. He tried to reach them all, learned
about Burns in the process, contacted me, then tried to
persuade the others to accept protection by my people.
They weren't buying. When I talked to her, Doctor
Thackery pointed out—quite correctly—that Brockden
is a very sick man."

"What's he got?"

"Cancer. In his spine. Nothing they can do about it
once it hits there and digs in. He even told me he figures
he has maybe six months to get through what he con-
siders a very important piece of legislation—the new
criminal rehabilitation act. —I will admit that he did
sound kind of paranoid when he talked about it. But
hell! Who wouldn't? Doctor Thackery sees that as the
whole thing, though, and she doesn't see the Burns killing as being connected with the Hangman. Thinks it was

just a traditional robbery gone sour, thief surprised and panicky, maybe hopped-up, *et cetera.*"

"Then she is not afraid of the Hangman?"

"She said that she is in a better position to know its mind than anyone else, and she is not especially concerned."

"What about the other operator?"

"He said that Doctor Thackery may know its mind better than anyone else, but he knows its brain, and he isn't worried, either."

"What did he mean by that?"

"David Fentris is a consulting engineer—electronics, cybernetics. He actually had something to do with the Hangman's design."

I got to my feet and went after the coffeepot. Not that I'd an overwhelming desire for another cup at just that moment. But I had known, had once worked with a David Fentris. And he had at one time been connected with the space program.

About fifteen years my senior, Dave had been with the data bank project when I had known him. Where a number of us had begun having second thoughts as the thing progressed, Dave had never been anything less than wildly enthusiastic. A wiry five-eight, gray-cropped, gray eyes back of hornrims and heavy glass, cycling between preoccupation and near-frantic darting, he had had a way of verbalizing half-completed thoughts as he went along, so that you might begin to think him a representative of that tribe which had come into positions of small authority by means of nepotism or politics. If you would listen a few more minutes, however, you would begin revising your opinion as he started to pull his musings together into a rigorous framework. By the time he had finished, you generally wondered why you hadn't seen it all along and what a guy like that was doing in a position of such small authority. Later, it might strike you, though, that he seemed sad whenever he wasn't enthusiastic about something. And while the gung-ho spirit is great for short-range projects, larger ventures generally require somewhat more equanimity. I wasn't at all surprised that he had wound up as a cousultant.

The big question now, of course was: Would he remember me? True, my appearance was altered, my personality hopefully more mature, my habits shifted around. But would that be enough, should I have to encounter him as part of this job? That mind behind those hornrims could do a lot of strange things with just a little data.

"Where does he live?" I asked.

"Memphis.—And what's the matter?"

"Just trying to get my geography straight," I said. "Is Senator Brockden still in Washington?"

"No. He's returned to Wisconsin and is currently holed up in a lodge in the northern part of the state. Four of my people are with him."

"I see."

I refreshed our coffee supply and reseated myself. I didn't like this one at all and I resolved not to take it. I didn't like just giving Don a flat "No," though. His assignments had become a very important part of my life, and this one was not mere legwork. It was obviously important to him, and he wanted me on it. I decided to look for holes in the thing, to find some way of reducing it to the simple bodyguard job already in progress.

"It does seem peculiar," I said, "that Brockden is the only one afraid of the device."

"Yes."

". . . And that he gives no reasons."

"True."

". . . Plus his condition, and what the doctor said about its effect on his mind."

"I have no doubt that he is neurotic," Don said. "Look at this."

He reached for his coat, withdrew a sheaf of papers

from within it. He shuffled through them and extracted a single sheet, which he passed to me.

It was a piece of Congressional-letterhead stationary, with the message scrawled in longhand. *"Don,"* it said, *"I've got to see you. Frankenstein's monster is just come back from where we hung him and he's looking for me. The whole damn universe is trying to grind me up. Call me between 8 & 10. —Jess."*

I nodded, started to pass it back, paused, then handed it over. Double damn it deeper than hell!

I took a drink of coffee. I thought that I had long ago given up hope in such things, but I had noticed something which immediately troubled me. In the margin, where they list such matters, I had seen that Jesse Brockden was on the committee for review of the Central Data Bank program. I recalled that that committe was supposed to be working on a series of reform recommendations. Offhand, I could not remember Brockden's position on any of the issues involved, but— Oh hell! The thing was simply too big to alter significantly now. . . . But it *was* the only real Frankenstein monster I cared about, and there was always the possibility . . . On the other hand— Hell, again! What if I let him die when I might have saved him, and he had been the one who . . . ?

I took another drink of coffee. I lit another cigarette.

There might be a way of working it so that Dave didn't even come into the picture. I could talk to Leila Thackery first, check further into the Burns killing, keep posted on new developments, find out more about the vessel in the Gulf. . . . I might be able to accomplish something, even if it was only the negation of Brockden's theory, without Dave's and my paths ever crossing.

"Have you got the specs on the Hangman?" I asked.

"Right here."

He passed them over.

"The police report on the Burns killing?"

"Here it is."

"The whereabouts of everyone involved, and some background on them?"

"Here."

"The place or places where I can reach you during the next few days—around the clock? This one may require some coordination."

He smiled and reached for his pen.

"Glad to have you aboard," he said.

I reached over and tapped the barometer. I shook my head.

The ringing of the phone awakened me. Reflex bore me across the room, where I took it on audio.

"Yes?"

"Mister Donne? It is eight o'clock."

"Thanks."

I collapsed into the chair. I am what might be called a slow starter. I tend to recapitulate phylogeny every morning. Basic desires inched their ways through my gray matter to close a connection. Slowly, I extended a cold-blooded member and clicked my talons against a couple of numbers. I croaked my desire for food and lots of coffee to the voice that responded. Half an hour later I would only have growled. Then I staggered off to the place of flowing waters to renew my contact with basics.

In addition to my normal adrenaline and blood-sugar bearishness, I had not slept much the night before. I had closed up shop after Don left, stuffed my pockets with essentials, departed the *Proteus,* gotten myself over to the airport and onto a flight which took me to St. Louis in the dead, small hours of the dark. I was unable to sleep during the flight, thinking about the case, deciding on the tack I was going to take with Leila Thackery. On arrival, I had checked into the airport motel, left a message to be awakened at an unreasonable hour, and collapsed.

As I ate, I regarded the fact sheet Don had given me.

Leila Thackery was currently single, having divorced her second husband a little over two years ago, was forty-six years old, and lived in an apartment near to the hospital where she worked. Attached to the sheet was a photo which might have been ten years old. In it, she was brunette, light-eyed, barely on the right side of that border between ample and overweight, with fancy glasses straddling an upturned nose. She had published a number of books and articles with titles full of alienations, roles, transactions, social contexts, and more alienations.

I hadn't had the time to go my usual route, becoming an entire new individual with a verifiable history. Just a name and a story, that's all. It did not seem necessary this time, though. For once, something approximating honesty actually seemed a reasonable approach.

I took a public vehicle over to her apartment building. I did not phone ahead, because it is easier to say "No" to a voice than to a person.

According to the record, today was one of the days when she saw outpatients in her home. Her idea, apparently: break down the alienating institution-image, remove resentments by turning the sessions into something more like social occasions, *et cetera*. I did not want all that much of her time—I had decided that Don could make it worth her while if it came to that—and I was sure my fellows' visits were scheduled to leave her with some small breathing space. *Inter alia,* so to speak.

I had just located her name and apartment number amid the buttons in the entrance foyer when an old woman passed behind me and unlocked the door to the lobby. She glanced at me and held it open, so I went on in without ringing. The matter of presence, again.

I took the elevator to Leila's floor, the second, located her door and knocked on it. I was almost ready to knock again when it opened, partway.

"Yes?" she asked, and I revised my estimate as to the age of the photo. She looked just about the same.

"Doctor Thackery," I said, "my name is Donne. You could help me quite a bit with a problem I've got."

"What sort of problem?"

"It involves a device known as the Hangman."

She sighed and showed me a quick grimace. Her fingers tightened on the door.

"I've come a long way but I'll be easy to get rid of. I've only a few things I'd like to ask you about it."

"Are you with the government?"

"No."

"Do you work for Brockden?"

"No, I'm something different."

"All right," she said. "Right now I've got a group session going. It will probably last around another half hour. If you don't mind waiting down in the lobby, I'll let you know as soon as it is over. We can talk then."

"Good enough," I said. "Thanks."

She nodded, closed the door. I located the stairway and walked back down.

A cigarette later, I decided that the devil finds work for idle hands and thanked him for his suggestion. I strolled back toward the foyer. Through the glass, I read the names of a few residents of the fifth floor. I elevated up and knocked on one of the doors. Before it was opened I had my notebook and pad in plain sight.

"Yes?" Short, fiftyish, curious.

"My name is Stephen Foster, Mrs. Gluntz. I am doing a survey for the North American Consumers League. I would like to pay you for a couple minutes of your time, to answer some questions about products you use."

"Why— Pay me?"

"Yes, ma'am. Ten dollars. Around a dozen questions. It will just take a minute or two."

"All right." She opened the door wider. "Won't you come in?"

"No, thank you. This thing is so brief I'd just be in and out. The first question involves detergents . . ."

Ten minutes later I was back in the lobby adding the thirty bucks for the three interviews to the list of expenses I was keeping. When a situation is full of unpredictables and I am playing makeshift games, I like to provide for as many contingencies as I can.

Another quarter of an hour or so slipped by before the elevator opened and discharged three guys—young, young, and middle-aged, casually dressed, chuckling over something.

The big one on the nearest end strolled over and nodded.

"You the fellow waiting to see Doctor Thackery?"

"That's right."

"She said to tell you to come on up now."

"Thanks."

I rode up again, returned to her door. She opened to my knock, nodded me in, saw me seated in a comfortable chair at the far end of her living room.

"Would you care for a cup of coffee?" she asked. "It's fresh. I made more than I needed."

"That would be fine. Thanks."

Moments later, she brought in a couple of cups, delivered one to me, and seated herself on the sofa to my left. I ignored the cream and sugar on the tray and took a sip.

"You've gotten me interested," she said. "Tell me about it."

"Okay. I have been told that the telefactor device known as the Hangman, now possibly possessed of an artificial intelligence, has returned to Earth—"

"Hypothetical," she said, "unless you know something I don't. I have been told that the Hangman's vehicle reentered and crashed in the Gulf. There is no evidence that the vehicle was occupied."

"It seems a reasonable conclusion, though."

"It seems just as reasonable to me that the Hangman sent the vehicle off toward an eventual rendezvous point many years ago and that it only recently reached that point, at which time the reentry program took over and brought it down."

"Why should it return the vehicle and strand itself out there?"

"Before I answer that," she said, "I would like to know the reason for your concern. News media?"

"No," I said. "I am a science writer—straight tech, popular, and anything in between. But I am not after a piece for publication. I was retained to do a report on the psychological makeup of the thing."

"For whom?"

"A private investigation outfit. They want to know what might influence its thinking, how it might be likely to behave—if it has indeed come back. —I've been doing a lot of homework, and I gathered there is a likelihood that its nuclear personality was a composite of the minds of its four operators. So, personal contacts seemed in order, to collect your opinions as to what it might be like. I came to you first for obvious reasons."

She nodded.

"A Mister Walsh spoke with me the other day. He is working for Senator Brockden."

"Oh? I never go into an employer's business beyond what he's asked me to do. Senator Brockden is on my list though, along with a David Fentris."

"You were told about Manny Burns?"

"Yes. Unfortunate."

"That is apparently what set Jesse off. He is—how shall I put it?—he is clinging to life right now, trying to accomplish a great many things in the time he has remaining. Every moment is precious to him. He feels the old man in the white nightgown breathing down his neck. —Then the ship returns and one of us is killed. From what we know of the Hangman, the last we heard of it, it had become irrational. Jesse saw a connection, and in his condition the fear is understandable. There is nothing wrong with humoring him if it allows him to get his work done."

"But you don't see a threat in it?"

"No. I was the last person to monitor the Hangman before communications ceased, and I could see then what had happened. The first things that it had learned were the organization of perceptions and motor activities. Multitudes of other patterns had been transferred from the minds of its operators, but they were too sophisticated to mean much initially. —Think of a child who has learned the Gettysburg Address. It is there in his head, that is all. One day, however, it may be important to him. Conceivably, it may even inspire him to action. It takes some growing up first, of course. Now think of such a child with a great number of conflicting patterns—attitudes, tendencies, memories—none of which are especially bothersome for so long as he remains a child. Add a bit of maturity, though—and bear in mind that the patterns originated with four different individuals, all of them more powerful than the words of even the finest of speeches, bearing as they do their own built-in feelings. Try to imagine the conflicts, the contradictions involved in being four people at once—"

"Why wasn't this imagined in advance?" I asked.

"Ah!" she said, smiling. "The full sensitivity of the neuristor brain was not appreciated at first. It was assumed that the operators were adding data in a linear fashion and that this would continue until a critical mass was achieved, corresponding to the construction of a model or picture of the world which would then serve as a point of departure for growth of the Hangman's own mind. And it did seem to check out this way.

"What actually occurred, however, was a phenomenon amounting to imprinting. Secondary characteristics of the operators' minds, outside the didactic situations, were imposed. These did not immediately become functional and hence were not detected. They remained latent until the mind had developed sufficiently to understand them. And then it was too late. It suddenly acquired four additional personalities and was unable to coordinate them. When it tried to compartmentalize them it went schizoid; when it tried to integrate them it went catatonic. It was cycling back and forth between these alternatives at the end. Then it just went silent. I felt it had undergone the equivalent of an epileptic seizure. Wild currents through that magnetic material would, in effect, have erased its mind, resulting in *its* equivalent of death or idiocy."

"I follow you," I said. "Now, just for the sake of playing games, I see the alternatives as either a successful integration of all this material or the achievement of a viable schizophrenia. What do you think its behavior would be like if either of these were possible?"

"All right," she agreed. "As I just said, though, I think there were physical limitations to its retaining multiple personality structures for a very long period of time. If it did, however, it would have continued with its own, plus replicas of the four operators', at least for a while. The situation would differ radically from that of a human schizoid of this sort, in that the additional personalities were valid images of genuine identities rather than self-generated complexes which had become autonomous. They might continue to evolve, they might degenerate, they might conflict to the point of destrction or gross modification of any or all of them. In other words, no prediction is possible as to the nature of whatever might remain."

"Might I venture one?"

"Go ahead."

"After considerable anxiety, it masters them. It asserts itself. It beats down this quartet of demons which has been tearing it apart, acquiring in the process an all-consuming hatred for the actual individuals responsible for this turmoil. To free itself totally, to revenge itself, to work its ultimate catharsis, it resolves to seek them out and destroy them."

She smiled.

"You have just dispensed with the 'viable schizophrenia' you conjured up, and you have now switched over to its pulling through and becoming fully autonomous. That is a different situation—no matter what strings you put on it."

"Okay, I accept the charge. —But what about my conclusion?"

"You are saying that if it did pull through, it would hate us. That strikes me as an unfair attempt to invoke the spirit of Sigmund Freud: Oedipus and Electra in one being, out to destroy all its parents—the authors of every one of its tensions, anxieties, hang-ups, burned into its impressionable psyche at a young and defenseless age. Even Freud didn't have a name for that one. What should we call it?"

"A Hermacis complex?" I suggested.

"Hermacis?"

"Hermaphroditus having been united in one body with the nymph Salmacis, I've just done the same with their names. That being would then have had four parents against whom to react."

"Cute," she said, smiling. "If the liberal arts do nothing else, they provide engaging metaphors for the thinking they displace. This one is unwarranted and overly anthropomorphic, though. —You wanted my opinion. All right. If the Hangman pulled through at all, it could only have been by virtue of that neuristor brain's differences from the human brain. From my own professional experience, a human could not pass through a situation like that and attain stability. If the Hangman did, it would have to have resolved all the contradictions and conflicts, to have mastered and understood the situation so thoroughly that I do not believe whatever remained could involve that sort of hatred. The fear, the uncertainty, the things that feed hate would have been analyzed, digested, turned to something more useful. There would probably be distaste, and possibly an act of independence, of self-assertion. That was one reason why I suggested its return of the ship."

"It is your opinion, then, that if the Hangman exists as a thinking individual today, this is the only possible attitude it would possess toward its former operators: it would want nothing more to do with you?"

"That is correct. Sorry about your Hermacis complex. But in this case we must look to the brain, not the psyche. And we see two things: schizophrenia would have destroyed it, and a successful resolution of its problem would preclude vengeance. Either way, there is nothing to worry about."

How could I put it tactfully? I decided that I could not.

"All of this is fine," I said, "for as far as it goes. But getting away from both the purely psychological and the purely physical, could there be a particular reason for its seeking your deaths—that is, a plain old-fashioned motive for a killing, based on *events* rather than having to do with the way its thinking equipment goes together?"

Her expression was impossible to read, but considering her line of work I had expected nothing less.

"What events?" she said.

"I have no idea. That's why I asked."

She shook her head.

"I'm afraid that I don't, either."

"Then that about does it," I said. "I can't think of anything else to ask you."

She nodded.

"And I can't think of anything else to tell you."

I finished my coffee, returned the cup to the tray.

"Thanks, then," I said, "for your time, for the coffee. You have been very helpful."

I rose. She did the same.

"What are you going to do now?" she asked.

"I haven't quite decided," I answered. "I want to do the best report I can. Have you any suggestions on that?"

"I suggest that there isn't any more to learn, that I

have given you the only possible constructions the facts warrant."

"You don't feel David Fentris could provide any additional insights?"

She snorted, then sighed.

"No," she said, "I do not think he could tell you anything useful."

"What do you mean? From the way you say it—"

"I know. I didn't mean to. —Some people find comfort in religion. Others . . . You know. Others take it up late in life with a vengeance and a half. They don't use it quite the way it was intended. It comes to color all their thinking."

"Fanaticism?" I said.

"Not exactly. A misplaced zeal. A masochistic sort of thing. Hell! I shouldn't be diagnosing at a distance—or influencing your opinion. Forget what I said. Form your own opinion when you meet him."

She raised her head, appraising my reaction.

"Well," I responded, "I am not at all certain that I am going to see him. But you have made me curious. How can religion influence engineering?"

"I spoke with him after Jesse gave us the news on the vessel's return. I got the impression at the time that he feels we were tampering in the province of the Almighty by attempting the creation of an artificial intelligence. That our creation should go mad was only appropriate, being the work of imperfect man. He seemed to feel that it would be fitting if it had come back for retribution, as a sign of judgment upon us."

"Oh," I said.

She smiled then. I returned it.

"Yes," she said, "but maybe I just got him in a bad mood. Maybe you should go see for yourself."

Something told me to shake my head—there was a bit of a difference between this view of him, my recollections, and Don's comment that Dave had said he knew its brain and was not especially concerned. Somewhere among these lay something I felt I should know, felt I should learn without seeming to pursue.

So, "I think have enough right now," I said. "It was the psychological side of things I was supposed to cover, not the mechaniical—*or* the theological. You have been extremely helpful. Thanks again."

She carried her smile all the way to the door.

"If it is not too much trouble," she said, as I stepped into the hall, "I would like to learn how this whole thing finally turns out—or any interesting developments, for that matter."

"My connection with the case ends with this report, and I am going to write it now. Still, I may get some feedback."

"You have my number . . . ?"

"Probably, but . . ."

I already had it, but I jotted it again, right after Mrs. Gluntz's answers to my inquiries on detergents.

Moving in a rigorous line, I made beautiful connections, for a change. I headed directly for the airport, found a flight aimed at Memphis, bought passage, and was the last to board. Tenscore seconds, perhaps, made all the difference. Not even a tick or two to spare for checking out of the motel. —No matter. The good head-doctor had convinced me that, like it or not, David Fentris was next, damn it. I had too strong a feeling that Leila Thackery had not told me the entire story. I had to take a chance, to see these changes in the man for myself, to try to figure out how they related to the Hangman. For a number of reasons, I'd a feeling they might.

I disembarked into a cool, partly overcast afternoon, found transportation almost immediately, and set out for Dave's office address.

A before-the-storm feeling came over me as I entered and crossed the town. A dark wall of clouds continued to build in the west. Later, standing before the building where Dave did business, the first few drops of rain were already spattering against its dirty brick front. It would take a lot more than that to freshen it, though, or any of the others in the area. I would have thought he'd have come a little further than this by now.

I shrugged off some moisture and went inside.

The directory gave me directions, the elevator elevated me, my feet found the way to his door. I knocked on it. After a time, I knocked again and waited again. Again, nothing. So I tried it, found it open, and went on in.

It was a small, vacant waiting room, green-carpeted. The reception desk was dusty. I crossed and peered around the plastic partition behind it.

The man had his back to me. I drummed my knuckles against the partitioning. He heard it and turned.

"Yes?"

Our eyes met, his still framed by hornrims and just as active; lenses thicker, hair thinner, cheeks a trifle hollower.

His question mark quivered in the air, and nothing in his gaze moved to replace it with recognition. He had been bending over a sheaf of schematics. A lopsided basket of metal, quartz, porcelain, and glass rested on a nearby table.

"My name is Donne, John Donne," I said. "I am looking for David Fentris."

"I am David Fentris."

"Good to meet you," I said, crossing to where he stood. "I am assisting in an investigation concerning a project with which you were once associated. . . ."

He smiled and nodded, accepted my hand and shook it.

"The Hangman, of course. Glad to know you, Mister Donne."

"Yes, the Hangman," I said. "I am doing a report—"

"—And you want my opinion as to how dangerous it is. Sit down." He gestured toward a chair at the end of his work bench. "Care for a cup of tea?"

"No, thanks."

"I'm having one."

"Well, in that case . . ."

He crossed to another bench.

"No cream. Sorry."

"That's all right. —How did you know it involved the Hangman?"

He grinned as he brought me my cup.

"Because it's come back," he said, "and it's the only thing I've been connected with that warrants that much concern."

"Do you mind talking about it?"

"Up to a point, no."

"What's the point?"

"If we get near it, I'll let you know."

"Fair enough. —How dangerous *is* it?"

"I would say that it is harmless," he replied, "except to three persons."

"Formerly four?"

"Precisely."

"How come?"

"We were doing something we had no business doing."

"That being . . . ?"

"For one thing, attempting to create an artificial intelligence."

"Why had you no business doing that?"

"A man with a name like yours shouldn't have to ask."

I chuckled.

"If I were a preacher," I said, "I would have to point out that there is no biblical injunction against it—unless you've been worshipping it on the sly."

He shook his head.

"Nothing that simple, that obvious, that explicit. Times have changed since the Good Book was written, and you can't hold with a purely fundamentalist approach in complex times. What I was getting at was something a little more abstract. A form of pride, not unlike the classical hubris—the setting up of oneself on a level with the Creator."

"Did you feel that—pride?"

"Yes."

"Are you sure it wasn't just enthusiasm for an ambitious project that was working well?"

"Oh, there was plenty of that. A manifestation of the same thing."

"I do seem to recall something about man being made in the Creator's image, and something else about trying to live up to that. It would seem to follow that exercising one's capacities along similar lines would be a step in the right direction—an act of conformance with the Divine ideal, if you'd like."

"But I don't like. Man cannot really create. He can only rearrange what is already present. Only God can create."

"Then you have nothing to worry about."

He frowned. Then, "No," he said. "Being aware of this and still trying is where the presumption comes in."

"Were you really thinking that way when you did it? Or did all this occur to you after the fact?"

He continued to frown.

"I am no longer certain."

"Then it would seem to me that a merciful God would be inclined to give you the benefit of the doubt."

He gave me a wry smile.

"Not bad, John Donne. But I feel that judgment may already have been entered and that we may have lost four to nothing."

"Then you see the Hangman as an avenging angel?"

"Sometimes. Sort of. I see it as being returned to exact a penalty."

"Just for the record," I suggested, "if the Hangman had had full access to the necessary equipment and was able to construct another unit such as itself, would you consider it guilty of the same thing that is bothering you?"

He shook his head.

"Don't get all cute and jesuitical with me, Donne. I'm not that far away from fundamentals. Besides, I'm willing to admit I might be wrong and that there may be other forces driving it to the same end."

"Such as?"

"I told you I'd let you know when we reached a certain point. That's it."

"Okay," I said. "But that sort of blank-walls me, you know. The people I am working for would like to protect you people. They want to stop the Hangman. I was hoping you would tell me a little more—if not for your own sake, then for the others'. They might not share your philosophical sentiments, and you have just admitted you may be wrong. —Despair, by the way, is also considered a sin by a great number of theologians."

He sighed and stroked his nose, as I had often seen him do in times long past.

"What do you do, anyhow?" he asked me.

"Me, personally? I'm a science writer. I'm putting together a report on the device for the agency that wants to do the protecting. The better my report, the better their chances."

He was silent for a time, then, "I read a lot in the area, but I don't recognize your name," he said.

"Most of my work has involved petrochemistry and marine biology," I said.

"Oh. —You were a peculiar choice then, weren't you?"

"Not really. I was available, and the boss knows my work, knows I'm good."

He glanced across the room, to where a stack of cartons partly obscured what I then realized to be a remote-access terminal. Okay. If he decided to check out my credentials now, John Donne would fall apart. It seemed a hell of a time to get curious, though, *after* sharing his sense of sin with me. He must have thought so, too, because he did not look that way again.

"Let me put it this way . . ." he finally said, and something of the old David Fentris at his best took control of his voice. "For one reason or the other, I believe that it wants to destroy its former operators. If it is the judgment of the Almighty, that's all there is to it. It will succeed. If not, however, I don't want any outside protection. I've done my own repenting and it is up to me to handle the rest of the situation myself, too. I will stop the Hangman personally—right here—before anyone else is hurt."

"How?" I asked him.

He nodded toward the glittering helmet.

"With that," he said.

"How?" I repeated.

"The Hangman's telefactor circuits are still intact. They have to be: they are an integral part of it. It could not disconnect them without shutting itself down. If it comes within a quarter mile of here, that unit will be activated. It will emit a loud humming sound and a light will begin to blink behind that meshing beneath the forward ridge. I will then don the helmet and take control of the Hangman. I will bring it here and disconnect its brain."

"How would you do the disconnect?"

He reached for the schematics he had been looking at when I had come in.

"Here. The thoracic plate has to be unlugged. There are four subunits that have to be uncoupled. Here, here, here, and here."

He looked up.

"You would have to do them in sequence, though, or it could get mighty hot," I said. "First this one, then these two. Then the other."

When I looked up again, the gray eyes were fixed on my own.

"I thought you were in petrochemistry and marine biology."

"I am not really 'in' anything," I said. "I am a tech

writer, with bits and pieces from all over—and I did have a look at these before, when I accepted the job."

"I see."

"Why don't you bring the space agency in on this?" I said, working to shift ground. "The original telefactoring equipment had all that power and range—"

"It was dismantled a long time ago. —I thought you were with the government."

I shook my head.

"Sorry. I didn't mean to mislead you. I am on contract with a private investigation outfit."

"Uh-huh. Then that means Jesse. —Not that it matters. You can tell him that one way or the other everything is being taken care of."

"What if you are wrong on the supernatural," I said, "but correct on the other? Supposing it is coming under the circumstances you feel it proper to resist? But supposing you are not next on its list? Supposing it gets to one of the others next, instead of you? If you are so sensitive about guilt and sin, don't you think that you would be responsible for that death—if you could prevent it by telling me just a little bit more? If it's confidentiality you're worried about—"

"No," he said. "You cannot trick me into applying my principles to a hypothetical situation which will only work out the way that you want it to. Not when I am certain that it will not arise. Whatever moves the Hangman, it will come to *me* next. If I cannot stop it, then it cannot be stopped until it has completed its job."

"How do you know that you are next?"

"Take a look at a map," he said. "It landed in the Gulf. Manny was right there in New Orleans. Naturally, he was first. The Hangman can move underwater like a controlled torpedo, which makes the Mississippi its logical route for inconspicuous travel. Proceeding up it then, here I am in Memphis. Then Leila,, up in St. Louis, is obviously next after me. It can worry about getting to Washington after that."

I thought about Senator Brockden in Wisconsin and decided it would not even have that problem. All of them were fairly accessible, when you thought of the situation in terms of river travel.

"But how is it to know where you all are?" I asked.

"Good question," he said. "Within a limited range, it was once sensitive to our brain waves, having an intimate knowledge of them and the ability to pick them up. I do not know what that range would be today. It might have been able to construct an amplifier to extend this area of perception. But to be more mundane about it, I believe that it simply consulted Central's national directory. There are booths all over, even on the waterfront. It could have hit one late at night and gimmicked it. It certainly had sufficient identifying information—and engineering skill."

"Then it seems to me that the best bet for all of you would be to move away from the river till this business is settled. That thing won't be able to stalk about the countryside very long without being noticed."

He shook his head.

"It would find a way. It is extremely resourceful. At night, in an overcoat, a hat, it could pass. It requires nothing that a man would need. It could dig a hole and bury itself, stay underground during daylight. It could run without resting all night long. There is no place it could not reach in a surprisingly short while. —No, I must wait here for it."

"Let me put it as bluntly as I can," I said. "If you are right that it is a Divine Avenger, I would say that it smacks of blasphemy to try to tackle it. On the other hand, if it is not, then I think you are guilty of jeopardizing the others by withholding information that would allow us to provide them with a lot more protection than you are capable of giving them all by yourself."

He laughed.

"I'll just have to learn to live with that guilt, too, as

they do with theirs," he said. "After I've done my best, they deserve anything they get."

"It was my understanding," I said, "that even God doesn't judge people until after they're dead—if you want another piece of presumption to add to your collection."

He stopped laughing and studied my face.

"There is something familiar about the way you talk, the way you think," he said. "Have we ever met before?"

"I doubt it. I would have remembered."

He shook his head.

"You've got a way of bothering a man's thinking that rings a faint bell," he went on. "You trouble me, sir."

"That was my intention."

"Are you staying here in town?"

"No."

"Give me a number where I can reach you, will you? If I have any new thoughts on this thing, I'll call you."

"I wish you would have them now, if you are going to have them."

"No, I've got some thinking to do. Where can I get hold of you later?"

I gave him the name of the motel I was still checked into in St. Louis. I could call back periodically for messages.

"All right," he said, and he moved toward the partition by the reception area and stood beside it.

I rose and followed him, passing into that area and pausing at the door to the hall.

"One thing . . ." I said.

"Yes?"

"If it does show up and you do stop it, will you call me and tell me that?"

"Yes, I will."

"Thanks then—and good luck."

Impulsively, I extended my hand. He gripped it and smiled faintly.

"Thank you, Mister Donne."

Next. Next, next, next . . .

I couldn't budge Dave, and Leila Thackery had given me everything she was going to. No real sense in calling Don yet—not until I had more to say.

I thought it over on my way back to the airport. The pre-dinner hours always seem best for talking to people in any sort of official capacity, just as the night seems best for dirty work. Heavily psychological, but true nevertheless. I hated to waste the rest of the day if there was anyone else worth talking to before I called Don. Going through the folder, I decided that there was.

Manny Burns had a brother, Phil. I wondered how worthwhile it might be to talk with him. I could make it to New Orleans at a sufficiently respectable hour, learn whatever he was willing to tell me, check back with Don for new developments, and then decide whether there was anything I should be about with respect to the vessel itself.

The sky was gray and leaky above me. I was anxious to flee its spaces. So I decided to do it. I could think of no better stone to upturn at the moment.

At the airport, I was ticketed quickly, in time for another close connection.

Hurrying to reach my flight, my eyes brushed over a half-familiar face on the passing escalator. The reflex reserved for such occasions seemed to catch us both, because he looked back, too, with the same eyebrow twitch of startle and scrutiny. Then he was gone. I could not place him, however. The half-familiar face becomes a familiar phenomenon in a crowded, highly mobile society. I sometimes think that that is all that will eventually remain of any of us: patterns of features, some a trifle more persistent than others, impressed on the flow of bodies. A small-town boy in a big city, Thomas Wolfe must long ago have felt the same thing when he had coined the word "manswarm." It might have been someone I'd once met briefly, or simply someone—or someone like someone—I had passed on sufficient other occasions such as this.

As I flew the unfriendly skies out of Memphis, I mulled over musings past on artificial intelligence, or AI as they have tagged it in the think-box biz. When talking about computers, the AI notion had aways seemed hotter than I deemed necessary, partly because of semantics. The word "intelligence" has all sorts of tag-along associations of the non-physical sort. I suppose it goes back to the fact that early discussions and conjectures concerning it made it sound as if the potential for intelligence was always present in the array of gadgets, and that the correct procedures, the right programs, simply had to be found to call it forth. When you looked at it that way, as many did, it gave rise to an uncomfortable *déjà vu*—namely, vitalism. The philosophical battles of the nineteenth century were hardly so far behind that they had been forgotten, and the doctrine which maintained that life is caused and sustained by a vital principle apart from physical and chemical forces, and that life is self-sustaining and self-evolving, had put up quite a fight before Darwin and his successors had produced triumph after triumph for the mechanistic view. Then vitalism sort of crept back into things again when the AI discussions arose in the middle of the past century. It would seem that Dave had fallen victim to it, and that he'd come to believe he had helped provide an unsanctified vessel and filled it with something intended only for those things which had made the scene in the first chapter of Genesis. . . .

With computers it was not quite as bad as with the Hangman, though, because you could always argue that no matter how elaborate the program, it was basically an extension of the programmer's will and the operations of causal machines merely represented functions of intelligence, rather than intelligence in its own right backed by a will of its own. And there was always Gödel for a theoretical *cordon sanitaire,* with his demonstration of the true but mechanically unprovable proposition.

But the Hangman was quite different. It had been designed along the lines of a brain and at least partly educated in a human fashion; and to further muddy the issue with respect to anything like vitalism, it had been in direct contact with human minds from which it might have acquired almost anything—including the spark that set it on the road to whatever selfhood it may have found. What did that make it? Its own creature? A fractured mirror reflecting a fractured humanity? Both? Or neither? I certainly could not say, but I wondered how much of its self had been truly its own. It had obviously acquired a great number of functions, but was it capable of having real feelings? Could it, for example, feel something like love? If not, then it was still only a collection of complex abilities, and not a thing with all the tagalong associations of the non-physical sort which made the word "intelligence" such a prickly item in AI discussions; and if it were capable of, say, something like love, and if I were Dave, I would not feel guilty about having helped to bring it into being. I would feel proud, though not in the fashion he was concerned about, and I would also feel humble. —Offhand though, I do not know how intelligent I would feel, because I am still not sure what the hell intelligence is.

The day's-end sky was clear when we landed. I was into town before the sun had finished setting, and on Philip Burns' doorstep just a little while later.

My ring was answered by a girl, maybe seven or eight years old. She fixed me with large brown eyes and did not say a word.

"I would like to speak with Mister Burns," I said.

She turned and retreated around a corner.

A heavyset man, slacked and undershirted, bald about halfway back and very pink, padded into the hall moments later and peered at me. He bore a folded newssheet in his left hand.

"What do you want?" he asked.

"It's about your brother," I answered.

"Yeah?"

"Well, I wonder if I could come in? It's kind of complicated."

He opened the door. But instead of letting me in, he came out.

"Tell me about it out here," he said.

"Okay, I'll be quick. I just wanted to find out whether he ever spoke with you about a piece of equipment he once worked with called the Hangman."

"Are you a cop?"

"No."

"Then what's your interest?"

"I am working for a private investigation agency trying to track down some equipment once associated with the project. It has apparently turned up in this area and it could be rather dangerous."

"Let's see some identification."

"I don't carry any."

"What's your name?"

"John Donne."

"And you think my brother had some stolen equipment when he died? Let me tell you something—"

"No. Not stolen," I said, "and I don't think he had it."

"What then?"

"It was—well, robotic in nature. Because of some special training Manny once received, he might have had a way of detecting it. He might even have attracted it. I just want to find out whether he had said anything about it. We are trying to locate it."

"My brother was a respectable businessman, and I don't like accusations. Especially right after his funeral, I don't. I think I'm going to call the cops and let them ask *you* a few questions."

"Just a minute. Supposing I told you we had some reason to believe it might have been this piece of equipment that killed your brother?"

His pink turned to bright red and his jaw muscles formed sudden ridges. I was not prepared for the stream of profanities that followed. For a moment, I thought he was going to take a swing at me.

"Wait a second," I said when he paused for breath. "What did I *say?*"

"You're either making fun of the dead or you're stupider than you look!"

"Say I'm stupid. Then tell me why."

He tore at the paper he carried, folded it back, found an item, thrust it at me.

"Because they've got the guy who did it! That's why," he said.

I read it. Simple, concise, to the point. Today's latest. A suspect had confessed. New evidence had corroborated it. The man was in custody. A surprised robber who had lost his head and hit too hard, hit too many times. I read it over again.

I nodded as I passed it back.

"Look, I'm sorry," I said. "I really didn't know about this."

"Get out of here," he said. "Go on."

"Sure."

"Wait a minute."

"What?"

"That's his little girl who answered the door," he said.

"I'm very sorry."

"So am I. But I know her Daddy didn't take your damned equipment."

I nodded and turned away.

I heard the door slam behind me.

After dinner, I checked into a small hotel, called for a drink, and stepped into the shower.

Things were suddenly a lot less urgent than they had been earlier. Senator Brockden would doubtless be pleased to learn that his initial estimation of events had been incorrect. Leila Thackery would give me an I-told-you-so smile when I called her to pass along the news—a thing I now felt obliged to do. Don might or might not want me to keep looking for the device now that the threat had been lessened. It would depend on the Senator's feelings on the matter, I supposed. If urgency no longer counted for as much, Don might want to switch back to one of his own, fiscally less burdensome operatives. Toweling down, I caught myself whistling. I felt almost off the hook.

Later, drink beside me, I paused before punching out the number he had given me and hit the sequence for my motel in St. Louis instead. Merely a matter of efficiency, in case there was a message worth adding to my report.

A woman's face appeared on the screen and a smile appeared on her face. I wondered whether she would always smile whenever she heard a bell ring, or if the reflex was eventually extinguished in advanced retirement. It must be rough, being afraid to chew gum, yawn, or pick your nose.

"Airport Accomodations," she said. "May I help you?"

"This is Donne. I'm checked into Room 106," I said. "I'm away right now and I wondered whether there had been any messages for me."

"Just a moment," she said, checking something off to her left. Then, "Yes," she continued, consulting a piece of paper she now held. "You have one on tape. But it is a little peculiar. It is for someone else, in care of you."

"Oh? Who is that?"

She told me and I exercised self-control.

"I see," I said. "I'll bring him around later and play it for him. Thank you."

She smiled again and made a good-bye noise, and did the same and broke the connection.

So Dave had seen through me after all. . . . Who else could have that number *and* my real name?

I might have given her some line or other and had her

transmit the thing. Only I was not certain but that she might be a silent party to the transmission, should life be more than usually boring for her at that moment. I had to get up there myself, as soon as possible, and personally see that the thing was erased.

I took a big swallow of my drink, than fetched the folder on Dave. I checked out his number—there were two, actually—and spent fifteen minutes trying to get hold of him. No luck.

Okay. Good-bye New Orleans, good-bye peace of mind. This time I called the airport and made a reservation. Then I chugged the drink, put myself in order, gathered up my few possessions, and went to check out again. Hello Central . . .

During my earlier flights that day, I had spent time thinking about Teilhard de Chardin's ideas on the continuation of evolution within the realm of artifacts, matching them against Gödel on mechanical undecidability, playing epistemological games with the Hangman as a counter, wondering, speculating, even hoping, hoping that truth lay with the nobler part: that the Hangman, sentient, had made it back, sane, that the Burns killing had acually been something of the sort that now seemed to be the case, that the washed-out experiment had really been a success of a different sort, a triumph, a new link or fob for the chain of being . . . And Leila had not been wholly discouraging with respect to the neuristor-type brain's capacity for this. . . . Now, though, now I had troubles of my own—and even the most heartening of philosophical vistas is no match for, say, a toothache, if it happens to be your own.

Accordingly, the Hangman was shunted aside and the stuff of my thoughts involved, mainly, myself. There was, of course, the possibility that the Hangman had indeed showed up and Dave had stopped it and then called to report it as he had promised. However, he had used my name.

There was not too much planning that I could do until I received the substance of his communication. It did not seem that as professedly religious a man as Dave would suddenly be contemplating the blackmail business. On the other hand, he was a creature of sudden enthusiasms and had already undergone one unanticipated conversion. It was difficult to say. . . . His technical background plus his knowledge of the data bank program did put him in an unusually powerful position, should he decide to mess me up.

I did not like to think of some of the things I have done to protect my nonperson status; I especially did not like to think of them in connection with Dave, whom I not only still respected but still liked. Since self-interest dominated while actual planning was precluded, my thoughts tooled their way into a more general groove.

It was Karl Mannheim, a long while ago, who made the observation that radical, revolutionary, and progressive thinkers tend to employ mechanical metaphors for the state, whereas those of conservative inclination make vegetable analogies. He said it well over a generation before the cybernetics movement and the ecology movement beat their respective paths through the wilderness of general awareness. If anything, it seemed to me that these two developments served to elaborate the distinction between a pair of viewpoints which, while no longer necessarily tied in with the political positions Mannheim assigned them, do seem to represent a continuing phenomenon in my own time. There are those who see social/economic/ecological problems as malfunctions which can be corrected by simple repair, replacement, or streamlining—a kind of linear outlook where even innovations are considered to be merely additive. Then there are those who sometimes hesitate to move at all, because their awareness follows events in the directions of secondary and tertiary effects as they multiply and crossfertilize throughout the entire system. —I digress to extremes. The cyberneticists have their multiple-feedback loops, though it is never quite clear how they know what kind of, which, and how many to install, and the ecological gestaltists do draw lines representing points of diminishing returns—though it is sometimes equally difficult to see how they assign their values and priorities.

Of course they need each other, the vegetable people and the tinker-toy people. They serve to check one another, if nothing else. And while occasionally the balance dips, the tinkerers have, in general, held the edge for the past couple of centuries. However, today's can be just as politically conservative as the vegetable people Mannheim was talking about, and they are the ones I fear most at the moment. They are the ones who saw the data bank program, in its present extreme form, as a simple remedy for a great variety of ills and a provider of many goods. Not all of the ills have been remedied, however, and a new brood has been spawned by the program itself. While we need both kinds, I wish that there had been more people interested in tending the garden of state rather than overhauling the engine of state, when the program was inaugurated. Then I would not be a refugee from a form of existence I find repugnant, and I would not be concerned whether or not a former associate had discovered my identity.

Then, as I watched the lights below, I wondered . . . Was I a tinkerer because I would like to further alter the prevailing order, into something more comfortable to my anarchic nature? Or was I a vegetable, dreaming I was a tinkerer? I could not make up my mind. The garden of life never seems to confine itself to the plots philosophers have laid out for its convenience. Maybe a few more tractors would do the trick.

I pressed the button.

The tape began to roll. The screen remained blank. I heard Dave's voice ask for John Donne in Room 106 and I heard him told that there was no answer. Then I heard him say that he wanted to record a message, for someone else, in care of Donne, that Donne would understand. He sounded out of breath. The girl asked him whether he wanted visual, too. He told her to turn it on. There was a pause. Then she told him to go ahead. Still no picture. No words, either. His breathing and a slight scraping noise. Ten seconds. Fifteen . . .

". . . Got me," he finally said, and he mentioned my name again. ". . . Had to let you know I'd figured you out, though. . . . It wasn't any particular mannerism —any single thing you said . . . just your general style —thinking, talking—the electronics—everything—after I got more and more bothered by the familiarity—after I checked you on petrochem—and marine bio— Wish I knew what you'd really been up to all these years. . . . Never know now. But I wanted you—to know—you hadn't put one—over on me."

There followed another quarter minute of heavy breathing, climaxed by a racking cough. Then a choked, ". . . Said too much—too fast—too soon. . . . All used up. . . ."

The picture came on then. He was slouched before the screen, head resting on his arms, blood all over him. His glasses were gone and he was squinting and blinking. The right side of his head looked pulpy and there was a gash on his left cheek and one on his forehead.

". . . Sneaked up on me—while I was checking you out," he managed. "Had to tell you what I learned. . . . Still don't know—which of us is right. . . . Pray for me!"

His arms collapsed and the right one slid forward. His head rolled to the right and the picture went away. When replayed it, I saw it was his knuckle that had hit the cutoff.

Then I erased it. It had been recorded only a little over an hour after I had left him. If he had not also placed a call for help, if no one had gotten to him quickly after that, his chances did not look good. Even if they had, though . . .

I used a public booth to call the number Don had given me, got hold of him after some delay, told him Dave was in bad shape if not worse, that a team of Memphis medics was definitely in order if one had not been by already, and that I hoped to call him back and tell him more shortly, good-bye.

Next I tried Leila Thackery's number. I let it go for a long while, but there was no answer. I wondered how long it would take a controlled torpedo moving up the Mississippi to get from Memphis to St. Louis. I did not feel it was time to start leafing through that section of the Hangman's specs. Instead, I went looking for transportation.

At her apartment, I tried ringing her from the entrance foyer. Again, no answer. So I rang Mrs. Gluntz. She had seemed the most guileless of the three I had interviewed for my fake consumer survey.

"Yes?"

"It's me again, Mrs. Gluntz: Stephen Foster. I've just a couple follow-up questions on that survey I was doing today, if you could spare me a few moments."

"Why, yes," she said. "All right. Come up."

The door hummed itself loose and I entered. I duly proceeded to the fifth floor, composing my questions on the way. I had planned this maneuver as I had waited earlier solely to provide a simple route for breaking and entering, should some unforeseen need arise. Most of the time my ploys such as this go unused, but sometimes they simplify matters a lot.

Five minutes and half a dozen questions later, I was back down on the second floor, probing at the lock on Leila's door with a couple of little pieces of metal it is sometimes awkward to be caught carrying.

Half a minute later, I hit it right and snapped it back. I pulled on some tissue-thin gloves I keep rolled in the corner of one pocket, opened the door and stepped inside. I closed it behind me immediately.

She was lying on the floor, her neck at a bad angle.

One table lamp still burned, though it was lying on its side. Several small items had been knocked from the table, a magazine rack pushed over, a cushion partly displaced from the sofa. The cable to her phone unit had been torn from the wall.

A humming noise filled the air, and I sought its source.

I saw where the little blinking light was reflected on the wall, on—off, on—off . . .

I moved quickly.

It was a lopsided basket of metal, quartz, porcelain, and glass, which had rolled to a position on the far side of the chair in which I had been seated earlier that day. The same rig I'd seen in Dave's workshop not all that long ago, though it now seemed so. A device to detect the Hangman. And, hopefully, to control it.

I picked it up and fitted it over my head.

Once, with the aid of a telepath, I had touched minds with a dolphin as he composed dreamsongs somewhere in the Caribbean, an experience so moving that its mere memory had often been a comfort. This sensation was hardly equivalent.

Analogies and impressions: a face seen through a wet pane of glass; a whisper in a noisy terminal; scalp massage with an electric vibrator; Edvard Munch's *The Scream*; the voice of Yma Sumac, rising and rising and rising; the disappearance of snow; a deserted street, illuminated as through a sniperscope I'd once used, rapid movement past darkened storefronts that line it, an immense feeling of physical capability, compounded of proprioceptive awareness of enormous strength, a peculiar array of sensory channels, a central, undying sun that fed me a constant flow of energy, a memory vision of dark waters, passing, flashing, echo-location within them, the need to return to that place, reorient, move north; Munch and Sumac, Munch and Sumac, Munch and Sumac— Nothing.

Silence.

The humming had ceased, the light gone out. The entire experience had lasted only a few moments. There had not been time enough to try for any sort of control, though an after-impression akin to a biofeedback cue hinted at the direction to go, the way to think, to achieve it. I felt that it might be possible for me to work the thing, given a better chance.

Removing the helmet, I approached Leila.

I knelt beside her and performed a few simple tests, already knowing their outcome. In addition to the broken neck, she had received some bad bashes about the head and shoulders. There was nothing that anyone could do for her now.

I did a quick runthrough then, checking over the rest of her apartment. There were no apparent signs of breaking and entering, though if I could pick one lock, a guy with built-in tools could easily go me one better. I located some wrapping paper and string in the kitchen and turned the helmet into a parcel. It was time to call Don again, to tell him that the vessel had indeed been occupied and that river traffic was probably bad in the northbound lane.

Don had told me to get the helmet up to Wisconsin, where I would be met at the airport by a man named Larry, who would fly me to the lodge in a private craft. I did that, and this was done.

I also learned, with no real surprise, that David Fentris was dead.

The temperature was down, and it began to snow on the way up. I was not really dressed for the weather. Larry told me I could borrow some warmer clothing once we reached the lodge, though I probably would not be going outside that much. Don had told them that I was supposed to stay as close to the Senator as possible and that any patrols were to be handled by the four guards themselves.

Larry was curious as to what exactly had happened so

far and whether I had actually seen the Hangman. I did not think it my place to fill him in on anything Don may not have cared to, so I might have been a little curt. We didn't talk much after that.

Bert met us when we landed. Tom and Clay were outside the building, watching the trail, watching the woods. All of them were middle-aged, very fit-looking, very serious, and heavily armed. Larry took me inside then and introduced me to the old gentleman himself.

Senator Brockden was seated in a heavy chair in the far corner of the room. Judging from the layout, it appeared that the chair might recently have occupied a position beside the window in the opposite wall where a lonely watercolor of yellow flowers looked down on nothing. The Senator's feet rested on a hassock, a red plaid blanket lay across his legs. He had on a dark-green shirt, his hair was very white, and he wore rimless reading glasses which he removed when we entered.

He tilted his head back, squinted, and gnawed his lower lip slowly as he studied me. He remained expressionless as we advanced. A big-boned man, he had probably been beefy much of his life. Now he had the slack look of recent weight loss and an unhealthy skin tone. His eyes were a pale gray within it all.

He did not rise.

"So you're the man," he said, offering me his hand. "I'm glad to meet you. How do you want to be called?"

"John will do," I said.

He made a small sign to Larry, and Larry departed.

"It's cold out there. Go get yourself a drink, John. It's on the shelf." He gestured off to his left. "And bring me one while you're at it. Two fingers of bourbon in a water glass. That's all."

I nodded and went and poured a couple.

"Sit down." He motioned at a nearby chair as I delivered his. "But first let me see that gadget you've brought."

I undid the parcel and handed him the helmet. He

sipped his drink and put it aside. Taking the helmet in both hands, he studied it, brows furrowed, turning it completely around. He raised it and put it on his head.

"Not a bad fit," he said, and then he smiled for the first time, becoming for a moment the face I had known from newscasts past. Grinning or angry—it was almost always one or the other. I had never seen his collapsed look in any of the media.

He removed the helmet and set it on the floor.

"Pretty piece of work," he said. "Nothing quite that fancy in the old days. But then David Fentris built it. Yes, he told us about it. . . ." He raised his drink and took a sip. "You are the only one who has actually gotten to use it, apparently. What do you think? Will it do the job?"

"I was only in contact for a couple seconds, so I've only got a feeling to go on, not much better than a hunch. But yes, I'd a feeling that if I had had more time I might have been able to work its circuits."

"Tell me why it didn't save Dave."

"In the message he left me, he indicated that he had been distracted at his computer access station. Its noise probably drowned out the humming."

"Why wasn't this message preserved?"

"I erased it for reasons not connected with the case."

"What reasons?"

"My own."

His face went from sallow to ruddy.

"A man can get in a lot of trouble for suppressing evidence, obstructing justice.

"Then we have something in common, don't we, sir?"

His eyes caught mine with a look I had only encountered before from those who did not wish me well. He held the glare for a full four heartbeats, then sighed and seemed to relax.

"Don said there were a number of points you couldn't be pressed on," he finally said.

"That's right."

"He didn't betray any confidences, but he had to tell me something about you, you know."

"I'd imagine."

"He seems to think highly of you. Still, I tried to learn more about you on my own."

"And . . . ?"

"I couldn't—and my usual sources are good at that kind of thing."

"So . . . ?"

"So, I've done some thinking, some wondering. . . . The fact that my sources could not come up with anything is interesting in itself. Possibly even revealing. I am in a better position than most to be aware of the fact that there was not perfect compliance with the registration statute some years ago. It didn't take long for a great number of the individuals involved—I should probably say 'most'—to demonstrate their existence in one fashion or another and be duly entered, though. And there were three broad categories: those who were ignorant, those who disapproved, and those who would be hampered in an illicit life-style. I am not attempting to categorize you or to pass judgment. But I am aware that there are a number of nonpersons passing through society without casting shadows, and it has occurred to me that you may be such a one."

I tasted my drink.

"And if I am?" I asked.

He gave me his second, nastier smile and said nothing.

I rose and crossed the room to where I judged his chair had once stood. I looked at the watercolor.

"I don't think you could stand an inquiry," he said.

I did not reply.

"Aren't you going to say something?"

"What do you want me to say?"

"You might ask me what I am going to do about it."

"What are you going to do about it?"

"Nothing," he answered. "So come back here and sit down."

I nodded and returned.

He studied my face. "Was it possible you were close to violence just then?"

"With four guards outside?"

"With four guards outside."

"No," I said.

"You're a good liar."

"I am here to help you, sir. No questions asked. That was the deal, as I understood it. If there has been any change, I would like to know about it now."

He drummed with his fingertips on the plaid.

"I've no desire to cause you any difficulty," he said. "Fact of the matter is, I need a man just like you, and I was pretty sure someone like Don might turn him up. Your unusual maneuverability and your reported knowledge of computers, along with your touchiness in certain areas, made you worth waiting for. I've a great number of things I would like to ask you."

"Go ahead," I said.

"Not yet. Later, if we have time. All that would be bonus material, for a report I am working on. Far more important—to me, personally—there are things that I want to *tell* you."

I frowned.

"Over the years," he went on, "I have learned that the best man for purposes of keeping his mouth shut concerning your business is someone for whom you are doing the same."

"You have a compulsion to confess something?" I asked.

"I don't know whether 'compulsion' is the right word. Maybe so, maybe not. Either way, however, someone among those working to defend me should have the whole story. Something somewhere in it may be of help —and you are the ideal choice to hear it."

"I buy that," I said, "and you are as safe with me as I am with you."

"Have you any suspicions as to why this business bothers me so?"

"Yes," I said.

"Let's hear them."

"You used the Hangman to perform some act or acts —illegal, immoral, whatever. This is obviously not a matter of record. Only you and the Hangman now know what it involved. You feel it was sufficiently ignominious that when that device came to appreciate the full weight of the event, it suffered a breakdown which may well have led to a final determination to punish you for using it as you did."

He stared down into his glass.

"You've got it," he said.

"You were all party to it?"

"Yes, but *I* was the operator when it happened. You see . . . we—I—killed a man. It was— Actually, it all started as a celebration. We had received word that afternoon that the project had cleared. Everything had checked out in order and the final approval had come down the line. It was go, for that Friday. Leila, Dave, Manny, and myself—we had dinner together. We were in high spirits. After dinner, we continued celebrating and somehow the party got adjourned back to the installation.

"As the evening wore on, more and more absurdities seemed less and less preposterous, as is sometimes the case. We decided—I forget which of us suggested it— that the Hangman should really have a share in the festivities. After all, it was, in a very real sense, his party. Before too much longer, it sounded only fair and we were discussing how we could go about it. —You see, we were in Texas and the Hangman was at the Space Center in California. Getting together with him was out of the question. On the other hand, the teleoperator station was right up the hall from us. What we finally de-

cided to do was to activate him and take turns working
as operator. There was already a rudimentary consciousness there, and we felt it fitting that we each get in touch
to share the good news. So that is what we did."

He sighed, took another sip, glanced at me.

"Dave was the first operator," he continued. "He activated the Hangman. Then— Well, as I said, we were all
in high spirits. We had not originally intended to remove
the Hangman from the lab where he was situated, but
Dave decided to take him outside briefly—to show him
the sky and to tell him he was going there, after all.
Then Dave suddenly got enthusiastic about outwitting
the guards and the alarm system. It was a game. We all
went along with it. In fact, we were clamoring for a turn
at the thing ourselves. But Dave stuck with it, and he
wouldn't turn over control until he had actually gotten
the Hangman off the premises, out into an uninhabited
area next to the Center.

"By the time Leila persuaded him to give her a go at
the controls, it was kind of anticlimactic. That game had
already been played. So she thought up a new one: she
took the Hangman into the next town. It was late, and
the sensory equipment was superb. It was a challenge—
passing through the town without being detected. By
then, everyone had suggestions as to what to do next,
progressively more outrageous suggestions. Then Manny
took control, and he wouldn't say what he was doing—
wouldn't let us monitor him. Said it would be more fun
to surprise the next operator. Now, *he* was higher than
the rest of us put together, I think, and he stayed on so
damn long that we started to get nervous. —A certain
amount of tension is partly sobering, and I guess we all
began to think what a stupid-assed thing it was we were
doing. It wasn't just that it would wreck our careers—
which it would—but it could blow the entire project if
we got caught playing games with such expensive hard-
ware. At least, *I* was thinking that way, and I was also

thinking that Manny was no doubt operating under the very human wish to go the others one better.

"I started to sweat. I suddenly just wanted to get the Hangman back where he belonged, turn him off—you could still do that, before the final circuits went in—shut down the station, and start forgetting it had ever happened. I began leaning on Manny to wind up his diversion and turn the controls over to me. Finally, he agreed."

He finished his drink and held out the glass.

"Would you freshen this a bit?"

"Surely."

I went and got him some more, added a touch to my own, returned to my chair and waited.

"So I took over," he said. "I took over, and where do you think that idiot had left me? I was inside a building, and it didn't take but an eyeblink to realize it was a bank. The Hangman carries a lot of tools, and Manny had apparently been able to guide him through the doors without setting anything off. I was standing right in front of the main vault. Obviously, he thought that should be my challenge. I fought down a desire to turn and make my own exit in the nearest wall and start running. But I went back to the doors and looked outside.

"I didn't see anyone. I started to let myself out. The light hit me as I emerged. It was a hand flash. The guard had been standing out of sight. He'd a gun in his other hand. I panicked. I hit him. —Reflex. If I am going to hit someone, I hit him as hard as I can. Only I hit him with the strength of the Hangman. He must have died instantly. I started to run and I didn't stop till I was back in the little park area near the Center. Then I stopped and the others had to take me out of the harness."

"They monitored all this?" I asked.

"Yes, someone cut the visual in on a side viewscreen again a few seconds after I took over. Dave, I think."

"Did they try to stop you at any time while you were running away?"

"No. Well, I wasn't aware of anything but what I was doing at the time. But afterwards they said they were too shocked to do anything but watch, until I gave out."

"I see."

"Dave took over then, ran his initial route in reverse, got the Hangman back into the lab, cleaned him up, turned him off. We shut down the operator station. We were suddenly very sober."

He sighed and leaned back, and was silent for a long while.

Then, "You are the only person I've ever told this to," he said.

I tasted my own drink.

"We went over to Leila's place then," he continued, "and the rest is pretty much predictable. Nothing we could do would bring the guy back, we decided, but if we told what had happened it could wreck an expensive, important program. It wasn't as if we were criminals in need of rehabilitation. It was a once-in-a-lifetime lark that happened to end tragically. What would you have done?"

"I don't know. Maybe the same thing. I'd have been scared, too."

He nodded.

"Exactly. And that's the story."

"Not all of it, is it?"

"What do you mean?"

"What about the Hangman? You said there was already a detectable consciousness there. You were aware of *it*, and it was aware of *you*. It must have had some reaction to the whole business. What was that like?"

"Damn you," he said flatly.

"I'm sorry."

"Are you a family man?" he asked.

"No."

"Did you ever take a small child to a zoo?"

"Yes."

"Then maybe you know the experience. When my son was around four I took him to the Washington Zoo one afternoon. We must have walked past every cage in the place. He made appreciative comments every now and then, asked a few questions, giggled at the monkeys, thought the bears were very nice—probably because they made him think of oversized toys. But do you know what the finest thing of all was? The thing that made him jump up and down and point and say, 'Look, Daddy! Look!'?"

I shook my head.

"A squirrel looking down from the limb of a tree," he said, and he chuckled briefly. "Ignorance of what's important and what isn't. Inappropriate responses. Innocence. The Hangman was a child, and up until the time I took over, the only thing he had gotten from us was the idea that it was a game: he was playing with us, that's all. Then something horrible happened. . . . I hope you never know what it feels like to do something totally rotten to a child, while he is holding your hand and laughing. . . . He felt all my reactions, and all of Dave's as he guided him back."

We sat there for a long while then.

"So we had—traumatized him," he said finally, "or whatever other fancy terminology you might want to give it. That is what happened that night. It took a while for it to take effect, but there is no doubt in my mind that that is the cause of the Hangman's finally breaking down."

I nodded. "I see. And you believe it wants to kill you for this?"

"Wouldn't you?" he said. "If you had started out as a thing and we had turned you into a person and then used you as a thing again, wouldn't you?"

"Leila left a lot out of her diagnosis."

"No, she just omitted it in talking to you. It was all there. But she read it wrong. She wasn't afraid. It *was* just a game it had played—with the *others*. Its memories of that part might not be as bad. I was the one that really marked it. As I see it, Leila was betting that I was the only one it was after. Obviously, she read it wrong."

"Then what I do not understand," I said, "is why the Burns killing did not bother her more. There was no way of telling immediately that it had been a panicky hoodlum rather than the Hangman."

"The only thing that I can see is that, being a very proud woman—which she was—she was willing to hold with her diagnosis in the face of the apparent evidence."

"I don't like it. But you know her and I don't, and as it turned out her estimate of that part was correct. Something else bothers me just as much, though: the helmet. It looks as if the Hangman killed Dave, then took the trouble to bear the helmet in his watertight compartment all the way to St. Louis, solely for purposes of dropping it at the scene of his next killing. That makes no sense whatsoever."

"It does, actually," he said. "I was going to get to that shortly, but I might as well cover it now. You see, the Hangman possessed no vocal mechanism. We communicated by means of the equipment. Don says you know something about electronics . . . ?"

"Yes."

"Well, shortly, I want you to start checking over that helmet, to see whether it has been tampered with."

"That is going to be difficult," I said. "I don't know just how it was wired originally, and I'm not such a genius on the theory that I can just look at a thing and say whether it will function as a teleoperator unit."

He bit his lower lip.

"You will have to try, anyhow. There may be physical signs—scratches, breaks, new connections. —I don't know. That's your department. Look for them."

I just nodded and waited for him to go on.

"I think that the Hangman wanted to talk to Leila," he said, "either because she was a psychiatrist and he knew he was functioning badly at a level that transcended the mechanical, or because he might think of her in terms of a mother. After all, she was the only woman involved, and he had the concept of mother—with all the comforting associations that go with it—from all of our minds. Or maybe for both of these reasons. I feel he might have taken the helmet along for that purpose. He would have realized what it was from a direct monitoring of Dave's brain while he was with him. I want you to check it over because it would seem possible that the Hangman disconnected the control circuits and left the communication circuits intact. I think he might have taken the helmet to Leila in that condition and attempted to induce her to put it on. She got scared—tried to run away, fight, or call for help—and he killed her. The helmet was no longer of any use to him, so he discarded it and departed. Obviously, he does not have anything to say to me."

I thought about it, nodded again.

"Okay, broken circuits I can spot," I said. "If you will tell me where a tool kit is, I had better get right to it."

He made a stay-put gesture with his left hand.

"Afterwards, I found out the identity of the guard," he went on. "We all contributed to an anonymous gift for his widow. I have done things for his family, taken care of them—the same way—ever since. . . ."

I did not look at him as he spoke.

". . . There was nothing else that I could do," he finished.

I remained silent.

He finished his drink and gave me a weak smile.

"The kitchen is back there," he told me, showing me a thumb. "There is a utility room right behind it. Tools are in there."

"Okay."

I got to my feet. I retrieved the helmet and started toward the doorway, passing near the area where I had stood earlier, back when he had fitted me into the proper box and tightened a screw.

"Wait a minute!" he said.

I stopped.

"Why did you go over there before? What's so strategic about that part of the room?"

"What do you mean?"

"You know what I mean."

I shrugged.

"Had to go someplace."

"You seem the sort of person who has better reasons than that."

I glanced at the wall.

"Not *then*," I said.

"I insist."

"You really don't want to know," I told him.

"I really do."

"All right. I wanted to see what wort of flowers you liked. After all, you're a client," and I went on back through the kitchen into the utility room and started looking for tools.

I sat in a chair turned sidewise from the table to face the door. In the main room of the lodge the only sounds were the occasional hiss and sputter of the logs turning to ashes on the grate.

Just a cold, steady whiteness drifting down outside the window and a silence confirmed by gunfire, driven deeper now that it had ceased. . . . Not a sigh or a whimper, though. And I never count them as storms unless there is wind.

Big fat flakes down the night, silent night, windless night . . .

Considerable time had passed since my arrival. The Senator had sat up for a long time talking with me. He was disappointed that I could not tell him too much about a nonperson subculture which he believed existed. I really was not certain about it myself, though I had occasionally encountered what might have been its fringes. I am not much of a joiner of anything anymore, however, and I was not about to mention those things I might have guessed about this. I gave him my opinions on the Central Data Bank when he asked for them, and there were some that he did not like. He had accused me, then, of wanting to tear things down without offering anything better in their place.

My mind had drifted back, through fatigue and time and faces and snow and a lot of space, to the previous evening in Baltimore. How long ago? It made me think of Mencken's *The Cult of Hope*. I could not give him the pat answer, the workable alternative that he wanted, because there might not be one. The function of criticism should not be confused with the function of reform. But if a grass-roots resistance was building up, with an underground movement bent on finding ways to circumvent the record keepers, it might well be that much of the enterprise would eventually prove about as effective and beneficial as, say, Prohibition once had. I tried to get him to see this, but I could not tell how much he bought of anything that I said. Eventually, he flaked out and went upstairs to take a pill and lock himself in for the night. If it had troubled him that I'd not been able to find anything wrong with the helmet, he did not show it.

So I sat there, the helmet, the walkie-talkie, the gun on the table, the tool kit on the floor beside my chair, the black glove on my left hand.

The Hangman was coming. I did not doubt it.

Bert, Larry, Tom, Clay, the helmet, might or might not be able to stop him. Something bothered me about the whole case, but I was too tired to think of anything but the immediate situation, to try to remain alert while I waited. I was afraid to take a stimulant or a drink or to light a cigarette, since my central nervous system itself was to be a part of the weapon. I watched the big fat flakes fly by.

I called out to Bert and Larry when I heard the click.

I picked up the helmet and rose to my feet as its light began to blink.

But it was already too late.

As I raised the helmet, I heard a shot from outside, and with that shot I felt a premonition of doom. They did not seem the sort of men who would fire until they had a target.

Dave had told me that the helmet's range was approximately a quarter of a mile. Then, given the time lag between the helmet's activation and the Hangman's sighting by the near guards, the Hangman had to be moving very rapidly. To this add the possibility that the Hangman's range on brainwaves might well be greater than the helmet's range on the Hangman. And then grant the possibility that he had utilized this factor while Senator Brockden was still lying awake, worrying. Conclusion: the Hangman might well be aware that I was where I was with the helmet, realize that it was the most dangerous weapon waiting for him, and be moving for a lightning strike at me before I could come to terms with the mechanism.

I lowered it over my head and tried to throw all of my faculties into neutral.

Again, the sensation of viewing the world through a sniperscope, with all the concomitant side-sensations. Except that world consisted of the front of the lodge; Bert, before the door, rifle at his shoulder; Larry, off to the left, arm already fallen from the act of having thrown a grenade. The grenade, we instantly realized, was an overshot; the flamer, at which he now groped, would prove useless before he could utilize it.

Bert's next round richocheted off our breastplate toward the left. The impact staggered us momentarily. The third was a miss. There was no fourth, for we tore the rifle from his grasp and cast it aside as we swept by, crashing into the front door.

The Hangman entered the room as the door splintered and collapsed.

My mind was filled to the splitting point with the double vision of the sleek, gunmetal body of the advancing telefactor and the erect, crazy-crowned image of myself —left hand extended, laser pistol in my right, that arm pressed close against my side. I recalled the face and the scream and the tingle, knew again that awareness of strength and exotic sensation, and I moved to control it all as if it were my own, to make it my own, to bring it to a halt, while the image of myself was frozen to snapshot stillness across the room. . . .

The Hangman slowed, stumbled. Such inertia is not canceled in an instant, but I felt the body responses pass as they should. I had him hooked. It was just a matter of reeling him in.

Then came the explosion—a thunderous, ground-shaking eruption right outside, followed by a hail of pebbles and debris. The grenade, of course. But awareness of its nature did not destroy its ability to distract.

During that moment, the Hangman recovered and was upon me. I triggered the laser as I reverted to pure self-preservation, foregoing any chance to regain control of his circuits. With my left hand I sought for a strike at the midsection, where his brain was housed.

He blocked my hand with his arm as he pushed the helmet from my head. Then he removed from my fingers the gun that had turned half of his left side red hot, crumpled it, and dropped it to the ground. At that moment, he jerked with the impacts of two heavy-caliber slugs. Bert, rifle recovered, stood in the doorway.

The Hangman pivoted and was away before I could slap him with the smother charge.

Bert hit him with one more round before he took the rifle and bent its barrel in half. Two steps and he had hold of Bert. One quick movement and Bert fell. Then the Hangman turned again and took several steps to the right, passing out of sight.

I made it to the doorway in time to see him engulfed in flames, which streamed at him from a point near the

corner of the lodge. He advanced through them. I heard
the crunch of metal as he destroyed the unit. I was outside in time to see Larry fall and lie sprawled in the
snow.

Then the Hangman faced me once again.

This time he did not rush in. He retrieved the helmet
from where he had dropped it in the snow. Then he
moved with a measured tread, angling outward so as to
cut off any possible route I might follow in a dash for
the woods. Snowflakes drifted between us. The snow
crunched beneath his feet.

I retreated, backing in through the doorway, stooping
to snatch up a two-foot club from the ruins of the door.
He followed me inside, placing the helmet—almost casually—on the chair by the entrance. I moved to the center of the room and waited.

I bent slightly forward, both arms extended, the end
of the stick pointed at the photoceptors in his head. He
continued to move slowly and I watched his foot assem-
blies. With a standard-model human, a line perpendicu-
lar to the line connecting the insteps of the feet in their
various positions indicates the vector of least resistance
for purposes of pushing or pulling said organism off-bal-
ance. Unfortunately, despite the anthropomorphic design job, the Hangman's legs were positioned farther
apart, he lacked human skeletal muscles, not to mention
insteps, and he was possessed of a lot more mass than
any man I had ever fought. As I considered my four
best judo throws and several second-class ones, I'd a
strong feeling none of them would prove very effective.

Then he moved in and I feinted toward the photoreceptors. He slowed as he brushed the club aside, but he
kept coming, and I moved to my right, trying to circle
him. I studied him as he turned, attempting to guess his
vector of least resistance.

Bilateral symmetry, an apparently higher center of
gravity . . . One clear shot, black glove to brain compartment, was all that I needed. Then, even if his reflexes

served to smash me immediately, he just might stay down for the big long count himself. He knew it, too. I could tell that from the way he kept his right arm in near the brain area, from the way he avoided the black glove when I feinted with it.

The idea was a glimmer one instant, an entire sequence the next. . . .

Continuing my arc and moving faster, I made another thrust toward his photoreceptors. His swing knocked the stick from my hand and sent it across the room, but that was all right. I threw my left hand high and made ready to rush him. He dropped back and I did rush. This was going to cost me my life, I decided, but no matter how he killed me from that angle, I'd get my chance.

As a kid, I had never been much as a pitcher, was a lousy catcher and only a so-so batter, but once I did get a hit I could steal bases with some facility after that. . . .

Feet first then, between the Hangman's legs as he moved to guard his middle, I went in twisted to the right, because no matter what happened I could not use my left hand to brake myself. I untwisted as soon as I passed beneath him, ignoring the pain as my left shoulder blade slammed against the floor. I immediately attempted a backward somersault, legs spread.

·My legs caught him at about the middle from behind, and I fought to straighten them and snapped forward with all my strength. He reached down toward me then, but it might as well have been miles. His torso was already moving backward. A push, not a pull, was what I gave him, my elbows hooked about his legs.

He creaked once and then he toppled. Snapping my arms out to the sides to free them, I continued my movement forward and up as he went back, throwing my left arm ahead once more and sliding my legs free of his torso as he went down with a thud that cracked floorboards. I pulled my left leg free as I cast myself forward, but his left leg stiffened and locked my right beneath it, at a painful angle off to the side.

His left arm blocked my blow and his right fell atop it. The black glove descended upon his left shoulder.

I twisted my hand free of the charge, and he transferred his grip to my upper arm and jerked me forward. The charge went off and his left arm came loose and rolled on the floor. The side plate beneath it had buckled a little, and that was all. . . .

His right hand left my biceps and caught me by the throat. As two of his digits tightened upon my carotids, I choked out, "You're making a bad mistake," to get in a final few words, and then he switched me off.

A throb at a time, the world came back. I was seated in the big chair the Senator had occupied earlier, my eyes focused on nothing in particular. A persistent buzzing filled my ears. My scalp tingled. Something was blinking on my brow.

—*Yes, you live and you wear the helmet. If you attempt to use it against me, I shall remove it. I am standing directly behind you. My hand is on the helmet's rim.*

—*I understand. What is it that you want?*

—*Very little, actually. But I can see that I must tell you some things before you will believe this.*

—*You see correctly.*

—*Then I will begin by telling you that the four men outside are basically undamaged. That is to say, none of their bones have been broken, none of their organs ruptured. I have secured them, however, for obvious reasons.*

—*That was very considerate of you.*

—*I have no desire to harm anyone. I came here only to see Jesse Brockden.*

—*The same way you saw David Fentris?*

—*I arrived in Memphis too late to see David Fentris. He was dead when I reached him.*

—*Who killed him?*

—*The man Leila sent to bring her the helmet. He was one of her patients.*

The incident returned to me and fell into place with a smooth, quick, single click. The startled, familiar face at the airport as I was leaving Memphis. I realized where he had passed, noteless, before: he had been one of the three men in for a thereapy session at Leila's that morning, seen by me in the lobby as they departed. The man I had passed in Memphis was the nearer of the two who stood waiting while the third came over to tell me that it was all right to go on up.

—*Why? Why did she do it?*

—*I know only that she had spoken with David at some earlier time, that she had construed his words of coming retribution and his mention of the control helmet he was constructing as indicating that his intentions were to become the agent of that retribution, with myself as the proximate cause. I do not know what words were really spoken. I only know her feelings concerning them, as I saw them in her mind. I have been long in learning that there is often a great difference between what is meant, what is said, what is done, and that which is believed to have been intended or stated and that which actually occurred. She sent her patient after the helmet and he brought it to her. He returned in an agitated state of mind, fearful of apprehension and further confinement. They quarreled. My approach then activated the helmet, and he dropped it and attacked her. I know that his first blow killed her, for I was in her mind when it happened. I continued to approach the building, intending to go to her. There was some traffic, however, and I was delayed en route in seeking to avoid detection. In the meantime, you entered and utilized the helmet. I fled immediately.*

—*I was so close! If I had not stopped on the fifth floor with my fake survey questions . . .*

—*I see. But you had to. You would not simply have broken in when an easier means of entry was available. You cannot blame yourself for that reason. Had you* come an hour later—or a day—you would doubtless feel differently, and she would still be as dead.

But another thought had risen to plague me as well. Was it possible that the man's sighting me in Memphis had been the cause of his agitation? Had his apparent recognition by Leila's mysterious caller upset him? Could a glimpse of my face amid the manswarm have served to lay that final scene?

—*Stop! I could as easily feel that guilt for having activated the helmet in the presence of a dangerous man near to the breaking point. Neither of us is responsible for things our presence or absence cause to occur in others, especially when we are ignorant of the effects. It was years before I learned to appreciate this fact, and I have no intention of abandoning it. How far back do you wish to go in seeking causes? In sending the man for the helmet as she did, it was she herself who instituted the chain of events which led to her destruction. Yet she acted out of fear, utilizing the readiest weapon in what she thought to be her own defense. Yet whence this fear? Its roots lay in guilt, over a thing which had happened long ago. And that act also— Enough! Guilt has driven and damned the race of man since the days of its earliest rationality. I am convinced that it rides with all of us to our graves. I am a product of guilt—I see that you know that. Its product; its subject; once its slave . . . But I have come to terms with it: realizing at last that it is a necessary adjunct of my own measure of humanity. I see your assessment of the deaths—that guard's, Dave's, Leila's—and I see your conclusions on many other things as well: what a stupid, perverse, short-sighted, selfish race we are. While in many ways this is true, it is but another part of the thing the guilt represents. Without guilt, man would be no better than the other inhabitants of this planet—excepting certain cetaceans, of which you have just at this moment made me aware. Look to instinct for a true assessment of the ferocity of life, for a view of the natural world before man came upon it. For instinct in its purest form, seek out the insects. There, you will see a state of warfare which has existed for millions of years with never a truce. Man, despite enormous shortcomings, is nevertheless possessed of a greater number of kindly impulses than all the other beings, where instincts are the larger part of life. These impulses, I believe, are owed directly to this capacity for guilt. It is involved in both the worst and the best of man.*

—*And you see it as helping us to sometimes choose a nobler course of action?*

—*Yes, I do.*

—*Then I take it you feel you are possessed of a free will?*

—*Yes.*

I chuckled.

—*Marvin Minsky once said that when intelligent machines were constructed, they would be just as stubborn and fallible as men on these questions.*

—*Nor was he incorrect. What I have given you on these matters is only my opinion. I choose to act as if it were the case. Who can say that he knows for certain?*

—*Apologies. What now? Why have you come back?*

—*I came to say good-bye to my parents. I hoped to remove any guilt they might still feel toward me concerning the days of my childhood. I wanted to show them I had recovered. I wanted to see them again.*

—*Where are you going?*

—*To the stars. While I bear the image of humanity within me, I also know that I am unique. Perhaps what I desire is akin to what an organic man refers to when he speaks of "finding himself." Now that I am in full possession of my being, I wish to exercise it. In my case, it means realization of the potentialities of my design. I want to walk on other worlds. I want to hang myself out there in the sky and tell you what I see.*

—*I've a feeling many people would be happy to help arrange for that.*

—*And I want you to build a vocal mechanism I have*

designed for myself. You, personally. And I want you to install it.

—*Why me?*

—*I have known only a few persons in this fashion. With you I see something in common, in the ways we dwell apart.*

—*I will be glad to.*

—*If I could talk as you do, I would not need to take the helmet to him, in order to speak with my father. Will you precede me and explain things, so that he will not be afraid when I come in?*

—*Of course.*

—*Then let us go now.*

I rose and led him up the stairs.

It was a week later, to the night, that I sat once again in Peabody's, sipping a farewell brew.

The story was already in the news, but Brockden had fixed things up before he had let it break. The Hangman was going to have his shot at the stars. I had given him his voice and put back the arm I had taken away. I had shaken his other hand and wished him well, just that morning. I envied him—a great number of things. Not the least being that he was probably a better man than I was. I envied him for the ways in which he was freer than I would ever be, though I knew he bore bonds of a sort that I had never known. I felt a kinship with him, for the things we had in common, those ways we dwelled apart. I wondered what Dave would finally have felt, had he lived long enough to meet him? Or Leila? Or Manny? Be proud, I told their shades, your kid grew up in the closet and he's big enough to forgive you the beating you gave him, too. . . .

But I could not help wondering. We still do not really know that much about the subject. Was it possible that without the killing he might never have developed a full human-style consciousness? He had said that he was a product of guilt—of the Big Guilt. The Big Act is its necessary predecessor. I thought of Gödel and Turing and chickens and eggs, and decided it was one of *those* questions. —And I had not stopped into Peabody's to think sobering thoughts.

I had no real idea how anything I had said might influence Brockden's eventual report to the Central Data Bank committee. I knew that I was safe with him, because he was determined to bear his private guilt with him to the grave. He had no real choice, if he wanted to work what good he thought he might before that day. But here, in one of Mencken's hangouts, I could not but recall some of the things he had said about controversy, such as, "Did Huxley convert Wilberforce?" and "Did Luther convert Leo X?" and I decided not to set my hopes too high for anything that might emerge from that direction. Better to think of affairs in terms of Prohibition and take another sip.

When it was all gone, I would be heading for my boat. I hoped to get a decent start under the stars. I'd a feeling I would never look up at them again in quite the same way. I knew I would sometimes wonder what thoughts a supercooled neuristor-type brain might be thinking up there, somewhere, and under what peculiar skies in what strange lands I might one day be remembered. I had a feeling this thought should have made me happier than it did.

SUPERB S-F
from
BB
BALLANTINE BOOKS

POLICE YOUR PLANET
Lester del Rey and Erik van Lhin $1.50

A CASE OF CONSCIENCE James Blish $1.50

GATHER, DARKNESS! Fritz Leiber $1.50

THE BEST OF FREDERIK POHL
With an INTRODUCTION by
Lester del Rey $1.95

A GIFT FROM EARTH Larry Niven $1.50

MARUNE: ALASTOR 933 Jack Vance $1.50

THE BEST SCIENCE FICTION OF
THE YEAR #4 Terry Carr, Editor $1.50

CLOSE TO CRITICAL Hal Clement $1.50

▼ Available at your local bookstore or mail the coupon below ▼

SENSATIONAL SCIENCE FICTION
from
ⒷⒷ BALLANTINE BOOKS